'Are we going to fight?' Rory's voice was low and unthreatening. She shook her head. Rory said, 'Do you realise, Meg Mackenzie, that we've been together for twelve hours? It's almost three in the morning.'

She looked at the clock. 'You came at three. The baby was born just before midnight, wasn't he? And we've been sitting here for two hours. Time you went home.'

'Is it? I've never spent so long with a woman before.' He was teasing her, but very gently, very tenderly. 'I have enjoyed it—very much. It could become habit-forming.' He stood up and took his jacket from the hook, wrapping his scarf twice around his neck. 'We never did make that dinner date, Meg. Do you think we could do it one day soon?'

Meg followed him to the door. The night outside was very still and dark, with only the constant whisper of the sea, as it lapped gently now on the beach outside Craigie House. A few stars showed between clouds, but there was no moon. Could it be love's light in his eyes? Oh, if only . . .

Lancashire born, Jenny Ashe read English at Birmingham, returning thence with a BA and RA—the latter being rheumatoid arthritis, which after barrels of various pills, and three operations, led to her becoming almost bionic, with two manmade joints. Married to a junior surgeon in Scotland, who was born in Malaysia, she returned to Liverpool with three Scottish children when her husband went into general practice in 1966. She had written non-stop after that—articles, short stories and radio talks. Her novels just had to be set in a medical environment, which she considers compassionate, fascinating and completely rewarding.

Jenny Ashe has written nine other Doctor Nurse Romances, the most recent being *Surgeon in the Clouds*, *Sister at Greyrigg* and *The Surgeon from San Agustin*.

CHAPTER ONE

THE SEA was slate grey, restless, threatening but not angry, like some huge monster stirring in its sleep. Meg Mackenzie sat on the window seat of Craigie House and looked out at the familiar beach just over the road, at the shining sand and the stark shape of the Black Rock jutting from the sea outside the harbour mouth. The sky was luminous after the Indian summer day, livid in the mid-time between day and night. Soon now the Fife fishermen would chug out from Brathay harbour—Murdoch McLeod and his brother Alan, Hamish Robertson, Donnie McCallum—lads who had been at school with Meg, following, the few who were left, the ways of their forefathers, seeking a small livelihood in the icy waters of the North Sea.

Meg turned to Grace Henderson, who sat gentle and calm in her wheelchair at Meg's elbow, so that she could help her with her meal while they both looked out through the lace curtains, the panorama of village life. Meg said, 'This was a wonderful place to build a house. You see the coast road half the way to Pittemweem. And you see the Harbour Lane and what goes on in the village. And you see the fishermen every evening. Did you choose to live here, Auntie?'

Grace chuckled. 'No, dear. I inherited the place from an uncle. But I do agree with you—not much goes on here that I don't know about. I'm never bored.' She put out a thin white hand and touched Meg's arm. 'But I'm not so sure about you. I feel life must be too flat for you. You spend all your time looking after me, with so few friends of your own age, and only Catriona and me for company.'

Meg picked up the cup and spooned the rest of the

5

broth for Grace with a competent nurse's hand. 'Now we've been through all that. I love it here. And I've got my squash, and the amateur theatre. And anyway, you know very well that I've had rather more than I expected from a certain friend of my own age.' She grinned, the genuine twinkle in her dark eyes making Grace smile too.

Grace said, 'Well, yes, there was that unpleasant young man . . .'

Meg said positively, 'And that was quite enough. I never want to see Rex Donaldson again. Talk about a love affair with himself! Typical. All surgeons think they're gods, Auntie.' And she helped Grace to a final mouthful, before wiping her lips gently with the napkin. 'There—good girl! That was good, wasn't it?'

'No one makes broth like Catriona.'

'I'll fetch the pudding.' Meg collected the mug and spoon from the tray. 'Oh, here you are, Caddy. Thank you, that was one of your best.' Catriona was already coming in with a plate of bread and butter pudding. 'I'll have to play an extra game of squash so as not to put on weight!'

Grace looked troubled. 'Squash isn't a substitute for living, my dear.' But when Meg wagged a finger at her she smiled again, her pale blue eyes loving. 'Come on, Catriona, sit here with us, and let's bet on whose boat comes first out of the harbour. I'll bet on Murdoch tonight.'

Meg shook her head, as she sat down again and pulled the curtain to one side. 'No takers, Auntie. Murdoch has his brother with him. They'll be faster than Hamish.'

Catriona said in her nasal accent, 'Donnie might have his daddy with him.'

'You think old Bill can help? He's more of a liability these days—Donnie only takes him for company.'

There was a roar outside—an approaching car on the coast road from Anstruther and Pittenweem. The three women took it for granted that they all craned their necks for a good look at it, at the occupant, and at the destination of any vehicle that passed Craigie House. Catriona stood up and gave a little jump of excitement. 'Would you take a look at that?' she exclaimed.

It was indeed a beauty—long, low and scarlet. Meg breathed, 'He's slowing up, Auntie.' They could see the handsome figure at the wheel now, as the open car slowed and came to a halt just at the far end of the garden hedge, where the berries on the holly were starting to turn red. He had jet black hair and a beard, and was wearing an Icelandic sweater. He turned away from them to look out to sea.

Catriona was whispering too. 'D'ye ken the driver, Miss Henderson?'

A sports car was a novelty to the three women alert behind the lace. Grace was tiny, crippled by a stroke, but still pretty, her blue eyes lively and just as interested in the young man below as the plump, slightly spotty Catriona, and bright cheerful Meg. Grace murmured, 'Look, he's getting out. He must have stopped to look at the view.' She looked at the other two with a cheeky grin. 'And he's giving us quite a view too! I wonder if he realises.'

The sun was behind him, but the young man put up his arm to shield his eyes from the brightness of the sea, as the first of the fishing boats nosed out of harbour and headed for Fife Ness. It was as though he was expecting them, and he stood mesmerised, as the four small trawlers edged out to the horizon as though posing for a picture postcard.

'Och there, Miss Henderson! We forgot to see who came first.'

Meg said half to herself, 'Hardly surprising. Who'd want to look at a few mouldy old boats when they could look at a car like that?'

Neither of the others pointed out that Meg wasn't looking at the car. There was only the gentle noise of the tide turning, and the cry of the gulls wheeling over the

harbour. Then Grace exclaimed, 'Mercy, it can't be!
He's in Africa.'

Meg turned sharply. 'Who is, Auntie? Do you know
him?'

'For a wee moment I thought it might be Rory.'

'Rory Henderson?' Meg felt a rush of warmth to her
face as she recalled Grace's nephew. Rugby captain,
he'd been, when she first fell in love with him, and she
was only thirteen and not even noticed by the big boys.
'He went to London to be a doctor, and never came
home,' she remembered.

'He came to visit before he left for the Sudan.' Grace
was peering now, her eyes struggling with the growing
twilight. 'A fine man he made. But he had no great beard
as that one has. He was broader too.'

Meg said, 'The Sudan is no the kind of place where
they get fat, Auntie.' She turned to look at the adopted
aunt. 'Rory would never turn up without telling you?'

'He might. He was always playing tricks.' The old face
softened, betraying a great affection. 'If only . . .'

There was nothing to be seen of the fishing boats now
except a couple of dim mast lights at the horizon. The
man had walked down to the beach for a better view.
Now he dropped his hand and turned slowly. Then he
looked straight up at the windows of Craigie House
—and all three women leaned back suddenly, although
he could not have seen them behind the lace curtain.
Unless he saw the movement, as Catriona hastily took a
step backwards.

Grace gave a nervous little giggle. 'Come away, Meg.'

But Meg was fascinated by the way the light caught at
the man's eyes—extraordinarily bright, as though the
sight of the fishing boats had moved him deeply. Then
she said, 'He's not going to the car—Auntie, he's
coming here!'

'Then 'tis Rory right enough—Rory Henderson come
home at last. To the door, Meg, and make him welcome.
Oh, God be praised, to see my dear boy before I go!'

Meg ran to the hallway and put on the light. Her heart bumped painfully, as memories of being told she was too young to play with the big ones jostled with other memories of when the little ones had been allowed to go along—to gather cockles maybe, or wild raspberries, or to make up the numbers at football on the beach . . . She opened the door. He had been just about to ring the bell, and now a smile split the black beard. 'Hello there.' He took the three steps in one stride and held out his hand. 'She saw me. God bless her, but I always knew Auntie Grace would know me when I came home.'

'She said to make you welcome.' His handshake was warm and strong, and took away Meg's nervousness. 'You're Rory, aren't you?'

He smiled again and turned back to her as she closed the door. 'And I'm sure I ought to know you too. But there was never anyone so pretty when I lived in Brathay.'

Meg met his admiring glance. 'Never mind. Come and see Auntie—but don't be distressed. She's had a stroke, and she's in a wheelchair. I look after her now.'

He had been about to push open the door of the drawing room, but he stopped and nodded before he went in. 'Thanks for warning me.' He flung open the door then, strode across the room, enfolded the tiny lady in his arms and said warmly, 'Well, lassie, you haven't changed a bit.' Meg liked him from that moment. What a change there was in Grace, from the agile jolly woman who had taught all the village to play the piano to the shrunken little body with one side of her almost useless. But Rory showed no distress, only gladness to be back.

Grace was too happy to argue. 'My dear, it's wonderful to see you, even though you gave me a bit of a shock. But I like this kind of shock. Just say you're going to stay a nice long time.'

'I'll be staying so long that you'll be glad to get rid of me!' he laughed. 'I'm taking a job with Dr Gregory for a few months, while I look around for a hospital post.'

'So you've passed through the phase of wanting to make some grand gesture with your life? Africa showed you that it doesn't need grand gestures, only lots of small people willing to give themselves.'

His face changed, and he stood up from where he had been kneeling at her side and sat on the window seat. 'Africa educated me.' His voice was brittle suddenly. 'I'll tell you about it some other time.' The room was quiet then, as Rory grappled with his memories. He went on, 'How come you were always so wise, without going further than the next county, Auntie?'

She smiled. 'Come and say hello to Catriona. She's my number one cook, and she bakes like an angel.'

Catriona had been gazing with her mouth open from the recesses of the room. Now she came forward and gave an awkward little curtsey, as though extreme respect were due to such a man. Rory shook her hand heartily. Caddy said, 'Shall I be putting the kettle on?'

Grace shook her head. 'No, Rory will have a wee drop of the best malt.' The girl brought the silver tray with its three bottles of finest malt whisky, and Rory poured one for himself.

'Here's to old times.' He turned to Meg. 'And to new acquaintances.'

'You'll be sick of the sight of me,' she smiled. 'I'm always at Dr Gregory's surgery for Auntie's pills.'

'That's nice.' He smiled back, and the blue of his eyes was as overwhelming as the ocean.

'Will you stay here, Rory?' asked Grace.

'I'm to stay with Dr Gregory at first. Mother won't be too pleased.'

'Your mother doesn't know you're here either?'

He grimaced. 'You know Mother. How is she?'

'Crotchety as ever.'

'She's always been jealous of you, Auntie. You were always the popular one. I suppose that sort of thing gets worse as one gets older. I don't intend to stay with her—and anyway, Pittemweem is much too far.' Rory sipped his whisky with appreciation. 'I must say I've developed an interest in the ageing process. I have some fairly revolutionary ideas about treatment I hope Greg will let me try out.'

Meg looked across sharply. 'What sort of ideas? Dr Gregory is wonderful with the old. It would be cruel to change. Not fair to them, and upsetting for everyone who looks after them.'

Rory met her accusing eyes. 'Meg Mackenzie. Yes, I could hardly expect any other reaction from you. You were always at the back, as I recall—timid. And I suppose I can't blame you. You still have a small-town mentality. You've had no chance to learn.'

Grace watched Meg intently, but Meg wasn't going to let Rory get away with insulting her, nephew or no nephew. 'I've had plenty of chance. I'm a qualified Sister and midwife. I just happen to know what's right for Brathay. You may have seen more of the big world, Rory Henderson, but a small-town mentality is the right one for a small town.'

Grace clapped her hands. 'Well said, Meg! What do you say to that, Rory?'

He relaxed. 'I won't argue with my favourite auntie on my first day home. And as she'll take your side, maybe I won't argue at all.'

Grace said quietly, 'Meg has been as good as a daughter to me. But you know I wouldn't take her side unless I thought she was right.'

Rory snapped his fingers. 'I remember now, Meg. You lived in Laurel Villa at the other end of town, and your father was Major Mackenzie. How are your parents?'

'Mother died.' Meg looked down, and decided he ought to know more if he was going to be her father's GP. 'Worn out with Father's nagging. I visit every week, but I remind him of Mother, so he gets irritated if I stay longer. That's why I'm so grateful to live here.'

'Bad-tempered old soldier, is he?' queried Rory. 'I've met some like that.'

'He has a reason—chest trouble. Dr Gregory's had some X-rays done, and warned me it could be cancer.'

'Who looks after him?'

'Lily Scroggie. She's been with the family for years, and she's the only person he trusts now.'

'Well, I hope he'll trust me.'

Meg looked at Rory with a plea in her eyes. 'Don't interfere, Rory! He's content the way he is. No new broom stuff on Dad—please?'

'All right.' Rory finished his whisky. Then with a slight smile he said, 'Small-town compromise.' His gaze was piercing and vaguely uncomfortable.

'You'll stay for some supper, Rory?'

'Thanks, but I must be off. Greg is expecting me.' He bent and kissed Grace. 'See you very soon Auntie.'

Meg said briefly, 'I'll see you out.' She followed his tall figure, the shoulders blocking out the light, as he towered a foot above her. He opened the door and went down one step—still taller than she was. She tried to be polite, although he had stirred up feeling within her that made her unsure of herself. 'Good night, then, Rory. I hope you enjoy coming home again.'

His smile was genuine then. 'Thanks, Meg Mackenzie. I hope you're not going to make things hard for me.'

'I might if I think it's right.' She faced him squarely and shook back her hair, putting it back behind her ears with one hand. He suddenly reached up and put his large hand against hers against her hair, so that she felt the warmth of his palm on her cheek. She reddened at the physical reaction it caused on her. All her repartee, her clever remarks deserted her. Rory and she stood for a moment in the deepening twilight, then he took his hand away, and she put hers selfconsciously to her side. It was shaking as she grasped the doorknob. She watched him run lightly along the path through the open gate to the scarlet streak of a car. He jumped in and started the engine.

He looked up as the engine roared and buckled his seat-belt, but this time he did not smile. He took his left hand from the gear lever and raised it almost in a salute. Then he pressed the accelerator, checked the road behind, and shot off along the deserted road towards Brathay village. Meg heard the car as it slowed to turn down Harbour Lane, where the surgery was. She heard the sound cease as he arrived.

That was no ordinary medical assistant, she was sure Dr Gregory would soon find out. She wondered if Brathay was ready for such a man . . . if *she* was. It might be traumatic. It would upset patients who were unused to changes. She shook her head, and a wry smile came to her lips as she walked back slowly to the drawing room. Whatever it would be, it would never be dull—not with Rory Henderson in residence.

Grace was sitting quietly in what they called her 'Whistler's Mother' pose. Meg sat down and tried to pretend her heart wasn't racing, her face still pink. She knew Grace's eyes were on her, and she sought desperately in her brain for something ordinary and conversational to say. But after the whirlwind who had just whipped them all with his vibrant personality and good looks, it was impossible, and the three of them sat in the light from one table lamp, wondering what had hit them.

Grace said, breaking the silence, 'Play to me, Meg.'

Meg went to the Steinway. It was lovingly kept, polished and tuned, though poor Grace herself could no longer play. Meg was only too conscious of her own lack of skill. 'Chopin? Mozart?' She leafed through some of their favourite music books.

'Play some Hebridean songs—the dark blue book. It's old, I know, but somehow, seeing that boy, it reminded me of his father—that boy, such a fine figure of a man, Meg. His father was a great singer of the old songs. Play the *Eriskay Love Lilt*, Meg.'

The summer evening drew to a close harmoniously, with the sweet if hesitant sounds of the piano through the open window, the rolling waters just outside, the gentle breeze and the murmuring of it in the tall pines at the back of the grey stone house. Before she took her up to bed, Meg sat on the rug by the embers of the small wood fire, talking over the day, as they often did. Meg asked, 'Do you see Rory as a country doctor, Auntie?'

Grace said softly, 'Rory always succeeded in what he set out to do.'

'I remember. We tiny kids looked up to him. I venerated him then. We all did—Hamish, Marian and Lindsay, Donnie and Murdoch and Alan—but then the senior boys were almost men to us.'

Grace smiled. 'So I see him still as a wee laddie, while you see him as an older wiser man. We must see which of us is nearer the truth.'

Meg's reply was almost a snort. 'Neither! He's just a young doctor with new-fangled ideas and plenty of confidence to carry them through.'

'Take me up, Meg. I'm very tired tonight.' And as Meg helped her to her room, washed and changed her and brushed her white hair, Grace rambled on about Rory. 'I can't help thinking, Meg, that it might be good for him to have a little opposition. His self-esteem is pretty high. Take him down a wee peg, just a wee one. You're the one with the personality to do it, dear.'

'Auntie, you know that's impossible. A new eligible man in Brathay? His head will be enormous by the time they've all flocked to meet him,' Meg giggled. 'And because he's your nephew, you'll get a whole new set of callers, wanting to find out more about him.'

Grace chuckled too. 'And don't you be winking at me over their heads like you did when the new minister came, Meg Mackenzie. I have to be dignified, even though we know they've only come to peep.'

While Grace and Catriona were going through the shopping list for the grocer next moring, Meg found that she was as nosy as anyone, creeping to the window when no one was looking, keeping an eye on the Harbour Lane turning, to see if folks had heard about the handsome new GP. She wondered how Rory had felt when he woke up in his own home town this fine morning, after so many years away. Small-town mentality . . . Did he mean it? Was it true? And if so, should she resent his comment, or be proud of it?

'You'll want to walk down with Catriona to the bakery, Meg?'

'No, thank you. I'm not one of the gawking sightseers. I'll go for a walk, though, if you'd like to be taken down the road to Jimmy Stewart's café for a breath of air?'

'Jimmy Stewart's is in the opposite direction,' said Grace.

'Exactly. Coming?'

Grace laughed. 'No indeed, Meg. I'll go along with Catriona. I like to hear the gossip and I don't mind who knows it! Come away, Caddy, we'll need to hurry if we want the fresh rolls.'

'And the fresh news!' shouted Meg, as the two of them set off into Brathay. Catriona was young, but she was a capable lass, though not very bright, and she loved being in sole charge of the wheelchair. Meg watched them till they turned into Harbour Lane, then she locked the front door and set off along the main road towards Jimmy Stewart's café, which was just the right distance between Brathay and Anstruther to attract custom from both communities.

As she approached, she noticed there was a workman outside, apparently stringing coloured light bulbs up outside the café. There was a new plate glass frontage too, and the paintwork was freshly touched up in a rather garish blue. Jimmy, a balding little man who always wore his kilt, as a gesture to the tourist trade, was standing outside, giving orders to Jock Galloway, the man up the ladder.

'Come into a fortune, Jimmy?' smiled Meg.

He turned with a proud grin. 'Nay, lass, I'm going modern. What do you think?'

Meg didn't want to hurt his feelings. 'This is for the tourists from the caravan site?'

'Aye. Do you realise there's no night club within miles? I've been missing out, Meg Mackenzie. Jim's caff is now the Scarlet Flamingo! Appeal to the young ones, as well as the visitors. Make my fortune in two years, what do you think?'

'Sounds just like downtown Las Vegas,' remarked Meg.

He beamed, delighted with her guarded reaction. 'OK, Jock, the Scarlet Flamingo it is. Start painting.' He admitted to Meg, 'I've just been to Gran Canaria, lass, and those café owners dinna miss a trick. They ken what tourists are. Well, they'll find that James Stewart isna far behind.'

Meg said warily, 'I hope you'll still make decent coffee, Jimmy.'

'Of course! But I've got a licence now—I'm officially a wine bar. Same food as before, but attract more customers.'

'Things are certainly not what they used to be,' she agreed. 'I used to come in here for a penny sweet and a drink of lemonade after school.'

'And liquorice sticks! Dinna worry, I still keep them all. The kids can still get their tooth rot from Jimmy.' He turned. 'I was forgetting—you want a coffee?' He led the way inside. 'I hear Rory Henderson is back in town. His auntie must be delighted. His ma went all funny, did she no?'

'She keeps herself to herself.' Flora Henderson, widow of Grace's beloved brother, was a strange woman. The two women had never been close, but they kept up appearances, by seeing each other once a week after kirk. As they had little in common they usually played bridge, roping in the minister, Alistair Reid, who was too nice to refuse, and the local dentist, a rather flashy widow from England called Caroline Forbes. Meg always hoped that they would all be there, because she had to make up the four in emergency, and she found it stultifyingly boring.

She sipped her coffee, between bangs from Jock and shouted instructions from Jimmy. She had no doubt the Scarlet Flamingo would do well, but it did seem rather a shame, to modernise to this extent. She caught sight of a newspaper on the stand where Jock was doing his sawing up of planks. The headline read 'Bike gangs terrorise small coast towns.' She shivered. Brathay was a small coast town.

'Hello there, Meg Mackenzie.'

She shot round at the masculine voice. But it was only Alistair Reid. He was a good soul; he certainly did a lot more for his flock than old Mr Carnegie had done, preaching hellfire and never visiting. 'Hello, Alistair. Doing the rounds?'

'Yes indeed. May I join you? This banging and clattering is a bit of a bar to the art of conversation.'

'I was just reading the headlines in that paper. This sort of place could turn into a den of vice, Alistair. Jimmy doesn't see it yet—just stands there with his bare knees, rubbing his hands and seeing pound signs in the air.'

'Ah yes, the love of money, root of all evil—I'm allowed to say that because I'm the minister.' He smiled and took a sip of his cappuccino. 'I've just met Miss Henderson's long-lost nephew.'

'Our Rory. What did you think of him?'

'Very nice motor. Very nice chap, actually, but he gave me the impression that he's out to wake us all up a little. Did you know him as a child, Meg?'

'Slightly. Older than I.' She wished she could stop her cheeks colouring at the old memories. 'Could be too big for his boots, but time will tell.'

'Oh, surely not. He said he'd be delighted to give a

talk in the Argyle Hall—about the Sudan. Says he's got a lot of pictures.'

'You don't waste time, do you?' Meg smiled up into the rather gangling minister's nice grey eyes.

The young man's face changed at her direct look, and she knew he was embarrassed at her familiarity. Yet it wasn't embarrassment but pleasure, as he said, 'You don't know what a delight it is to run into you like this. 'You're usually so busy when we meet.'

Meg looked at her watch. 'I ought to be getting back.'

'I'll walk with you.' Alistair drank down the rest of his coffee very quickly. 'I haven't been to see your father this week. How is he, Meg?'

They walked along the road together, the sun dancing on the sea. This used to be a main road, but most traffic used the motorways now, and the way through the villages was nice and quiet, except at the height of the summer. Meg opened her heart to the young minister; he of all people could understand her home life. 'Mother was so sweet and gentle, she was turned into a doormat. That must be why I'm so aggressive: I don't ever intend to be treated as she was.'

Alistair said wisely, 'Most of today's girls feel that. There's never been any harm in standing up for yourself, no harm at all.'

There was a cheeky toot on an old car horn, and they stood to the side to see who was coming so noisily. It was Jessie Peebles, the district nurse, chugging along in her ancient Land Rover. 'Hello, Meg. Morning, Mr Reid. Sorry to hoot at you, but my steering's none too sure, and I'd hate to send you both for a swim in the North Sea!'

'Hi, Jessie. Nethergate Grange this morning, then?'

'Nethergate Grange every morning just now. It's a grand wee place, though. I only hope they have room for me when my time comes.' Jessie wound the window down more. 'I've just been to your dad, Meggie lass.'

Alistair took a step towards Meg, and she felt his hand

steadying her, his breath on the back of her head. Her
heart tugged. Alistair was so understanding. Even in her
father's grave illness, he didn't want Meg to nurse him.
She said, 'Why did you go? Did he call?'

'No, he would never do that. It was young Dr Henderson—insisted I go with him to assess the need. Quite a
live wire, our new doctor. Fun, too, don't you think,
Meg? He told me he'd met you last night, and that he
remembered what a timid little girl you used to be.'

Meg's lips set in a thin line. 'A bit too much of a good
thing, young Dr Rory. First morning, and he visits a man
who needs no visit? Father gets het up enough, without
getting calls he's no expecting.'

Jessie grinned. 'Och, it's no my fault. I do what the
doctors tell me.'

'I'm sorry. I'm not cross at you, Jessie,' said Meg, 'But
that Rory—he just ruffles feathers wherever he goes.
Brathay can do without his type of meddling.'

'Hey, lassie, you've gone quite pink!'

Meg grinned rather ruefully. 'I must take after my
father after all—quick temper. But Rory annoyed me
—he has a way of talking that sounds as though he's
condescending—makes folk feel inferior, the way he
does it . . .'

'Well,' Jessie's plump face was intelligent as she
leaned her elbow out of the window, 'Well, he probably
does know a lot more about the world than we do. He's
travelled a lot further.' She was always big-hearted, was
Jessie. 'I must be off. Are you going to Dr Henderson's
lecture next week, Meg?'

'Grace and I always go to the Argyle Hall. What's the
lecture on?' It was true. Most of the village attended the
Argyle Hall; it was the general meeting place and gossip
centre.

'Experiences in the Sudan. I believe he's collecting for
famine relief, isn't he, Mr Reid?'

'That's right,' Alistair agreed.

Meg shrugged. 'We'll be there. But—' she smoothed

her blown hair back behind her ears—and suddenly remembered the touch of Rory's hand on hers as she did just that—'if you want my opinion, I think he's arrogant, opinionated and far too cocky for his own good.'

Jessie hooted with laughter—so much so that Meg looked puzzled. Jessie put the car into gear and released the handbrake. 'I didna ken you liked him that much!' And she drove off, still laughing, showing off the dimples in her jolly face. Meg turned to Alistair. He too was watching her. There was a knowing look in his gentle eyes, and an expression on his face that was not a smile.

'But I don't . . .' There was no point in going on. She turned and started walking back to the village, with Alistair having no trouble keeping up with her fast pace, with his long legs. The sea still sparkled in the sun, the birds sang, but there was silence between the girl and the man, as though they had run out of conversation, and were busy with their own thoughts.

As they neared Craigie House, there was a familiar roar from Harbour Lane. Meg knew what it was, and kept her face determinedly out to sea as the red sports car turned left and passed them as the new doctor started on his rounds. He didn't hoot his horn, but Alistair saw him, and raised an arm in salute. 'It's Dr Henderson.' But by the time Meg turned, the red car was far past.

'That wasn't very friendly of you, Meg.' But before he had finished the sentence, Meg had run up the steps, and pushed open the door, closing it behind her with a little slam.

After she had regained her composure, she joined Grace in the drawing room. 'You should have come with us, Meg,' said Grace.

'I enjoyed my morning. I came back with the minister.'

Grace nodded. 'Very nice. But you would have been interested in the way Mrs Forbes suddenly developed an urgent illness.'

'Caroline Forbes went to the surgery?'

'She was very determined to be among the first to greet Rory. In her glad rags too—you know what a smart woman she can be. She's made sure Rory's invited for Sunday bridge. You'll have to entertain the minister, Meg.'

Meg tossed her head. 'It will be a pleasure,' she said. She wanted Rory to be very sure that Meg Mackenzie was no longer one of his devoted followers. What better way than to devote her time to chatting to Alistair, while the others bored themselves silly with bridge?

CHAPTER TWO

THOSE in the village who had not been able to invent a medical reason for going to the surgery to see the new doctor made sure they made their way to the kirk on Sunday morning. Meg and Grace exchanged a secret smile at the exceptionally large congregation. They had expected it. And indeed, Meg herself had spent rather longer than usual deciding what to wear. And a most delicious smell came from the kitchen, as Catriona did her best to prepare a lunch for Rory Henderson and his mother, Flora.

Meg usually dressed Grace first, leaving her sitting in the drawing room with the Sunday paper while she herself threw on the nearest decent dress. This Sunday Meg rifled through the wardrobe twice, and felt dissatisfied at what she saw there. 'Small-town rubbish,' she muttered to herself. Then her face flamed as she realised what she had said. 'What does it matter anyway! I'm going to Laurel Villa. I won't be here for lunch.' And she regretted that very much, because the roast was sending up signals of excellence, and because she knew the vegetables would be fresh from the garden, and the potatoes roasted to perfection.

Then she wondered if Caroline Forbes would be at the kirk, and decided that Caroline wouldn't miss it for worlds. She enjoyed being looked at, and indeed, Meg had to admit that she was usually the only lady worth looking at. They had felt sorry for Caroline when they heard that she had been married for only six months before her husband died of leukaemia very suddenly. But she had played on her tragedy, and tried to walk down the aisle always with a look of noble suffering on her pretty face. She had also been left a lot of money, and flew off regularly to the Azores or Crete or Los Angeles for a break.

Meg decided on her long-sleeved blue cotton sprigged with darker blue roses. It had a fashionable full longish skirt, and a high neck, but Meg felt it made her look like a Victorian governess, just when she wished she could look gay and pretty and carefree. However, as she pushed the wheelchair into the shadow of the kirk door, she bent her head so that her hair curtained her face, and apologised to God for caring so much about her appearance.

All the same, it was a sin many of the ladies of the parish had committed that bright September morning, as the kirk filled, and Caroline Forbes swept down the aisle in a close-fitting crimson dress, high heels and a small chic black hat, huge rubies glittering in her ears. Grace was being very wicked, by giving Meg sidelong glances, and she had to force herself not to giggle.

Alistar wandered about the congregation, chatting to some as he made his unassuming way towards the altar. He modified the atmosphere of suppressed excitement by his simple goodness, and Meg warmed to him, remembering how he had stood so close and so supportive that day on the coast road. He was unchanging, unaffected by custom or by fashion. He was not demonstrative about his faith, or fearful as the last minister had been. It was hardly possible to listen to him without being moved by his own total contentment, his certainty that he had found the only right way to go through this troubled world. For a few moments Meg thought even Caroline must have forgotten about making an impression, and Alistair spoke in his gentle Scots burr, making no attempt to be anything but himself.

There was no sign of Rory Henderson. But then during the first hymn, people began to turn round and stare, or drop things and pretend to pick them up so that they could peep. Rory had confounded them all by coming late with his little bent mother, and sitting right at the back. The congregation then looked steadily to the front, burning inside at his inconsiderate behaviour at not sitting in Mistress Henderson's usual pew near the front.

Grace whispered, 'I bet they all want to talk to Flora this morning.'

Meg looked down, looking even more like a Victorian miss, and hid a smile. 'It makes no difference to me.'

Then Grace caught her eye again. 'I've been young myself, you know.' And she turned demurely to her prayer book as Meg gave her a hard stare before softening into another smile. Grace hadn't missed her extra care with her dressing, her inability to sit still, and the studied way she kept her face to the front while all the rustling and whispering went on. 'Small-town mentality' rankled in her brain. Well, he was part of that small town now, no doubt extremely amused at the attention he was getting. Meg straightened her shoulders, determined not to show the slightest interest as she made her way out of the kirk.

The final benediction over, Meg knelt a little longer, wishing she could put into words what she wanted to pray for. So she prayed for Grace, as usual—the one person in Brathay she was truly grateful to, not just for a job, but for a home and friendship and understanding. She prayed for her father too, deeply and sincerely—if he could just be in a good mood when she called, that would mean a whole week free from guilt feelings and worry. And her thoughts strayed to her mother, how she had suffered so bravely under this tyrant, and sought release in death.

She sat up to some bright but rather inaccurate Bach played on the chesty organ by Mr Millar. She settled Grace in her chair and pushed her slowly up the aisle, knowing that the doorway would be packed with folk standing around gossiping. Grace turned her head to give her another wink, when they spotted Flora Henderson the centre of attention, because of the good looks of the stranger whose arm she clung to. Everyone wanted to shake Flora by the hand that morning, and pretend to be astonished that she was not alone as usual—as though they had not been talking about Rory non-stop since the moment he arrived in the village in his scarlet bullet of a car.

Meg waited patiently, chatting to Grace, and to Miss MacFarlane, the retired schoolteacher who was Grace's best friend. Soon the crowd would have to disperse, Flora would take over the wheelchair, and the family would go back to Craigie House for lunch, while Meg walked along the main street to her father's sparser meal at Laurel Villa. 'It's a longer wait than usual, Auntie,' she remarked.'

'It's a fine day, dear—no hurry. I'd just like to thank Alistair for his sermon. He speaks very well, that boy. Your father won't be waiting?'

'No, we have plenty of time. You'll telephone if you need me?'

'I will. Your father must have his share of you, Meg. Give him my regards. Tell him the raspberries will be ready next week, and I'll be sending him a basket.'

'I'll tell them. Mrs Scroggie'll be delighted,' said Meg.

Then it was their turn, and Alistair came to shake them by the hand with natural courtesy, before bending and saying rather wickedly to Grace, 'I'm afraid I'm not the most popular boy today.'

Grace chuckled. 'Rory's a novelty, dear. They'll soon tire of making a fuss of him, specially when they find out some of his new ideas!'

Alistair had only been joking. 'I hope they won't for a wee while. I'm counting on his popular appeal to give us a good turnout and collection at the Argyle Hall next week.'

Grace nodded, businesslike. 'Oh, they'll come to that, no doubt of it.'

As the small groups finally began to disperse, Meg noticed without surprise that Caroline Forbes was one of the group closest to Flora and Rory. And there was little doubt that Rory was finding her conversation a little more to his liking than some of the matrons of the village. Her lustrous dark eyes were upon him as though he spoke words of pure gold. The rubies in her ears glistened even brighter in the sunshine, and she stood out, the crimson of her dress against the dark green of the ecclesiastical yews by the kirk door. She was telling Rory how much she enjoyed bridge.

Meg felt left out. She wasn't awfully good at bridge —probably because it bored her to sit for so long at a table. But now she could hear the words in her head —small-town girl. Small-town mentality. Small-town mind . . . It didn't really matter, did it? She had never made a fool of herself over men before, Rex Donaldson excepted. She had never before made any special attempt to be noticed. Suddenly she wanted to. She wanted to be dramatic and outstanding. She wanted that masculine creature to be unable to look away because of her beauty, be speechless with admiration at her conversation and aplomb! ·

Yet she stood at the back of the group, listening now brazenly to Rory and Caroline talking. It appeared they had acquaintances in common from university days. And those rubies flashed each time she moved her head. Her eyes were even more beautiful when enlivened by a new and handsome companion. Meg looked down, and remembered her own moment of contact—the moment when he had touched her hair, and those blue eyes had been for a few seconds hers.

Flora Henderson noticed Meg at last. 'There's no need for you to hang around, Meg. I'll take the wheel-chair.'

Meg had been hoping at least for a word or two with Rory. She had not expected to be dismissed so rudely or so quickly. She wanted to listen and to learn, to find out from Caroline what subjects interested him, and how to speak—to imitate Caroline's toss of the head, and her sparkling manner. But at Flora's remark, she let go of the wheelchair as though of an umbilical cord, and turned to go, unwilling even to raise her voice to say goodbye to Rory. 'Very well. See you this evening, Auntie.'

But at that very moment Rory looked up, detached himself from Caroline's painted fingers, and was walking after her along the kirk path. 'I'll walk to the gate with you, Meg. Do you always visit on Sundays?'

She realised he only wanted to talk about her father —his patient. She wasn't really disappointed. She had expected no more. 'Yes. Mrs Scroggie cooks lunch for us. But his appetite isn't what it was these days.'

They had reached the wooden gate all too soon. They stopped, and she waited for some medical advice. But Rory said gently, 'You're taller than I remember, Meg Mackenzie. But you're still wee—and shy. I didn't know you very well, did I?'

'You didn't know me at all. There was nothing to know at thirteen.'

'And now?' His smile was genuine, and it was all for her. Now was the time to sparkle as Caroline had done. But she could think of nothing sparkling to say. Rory answered for her. 'I shall just have to find out for myself.'

Meg said, haltingly, 'Rory, you do understand that I can't look after my father—how I annoy him if I stay too long? You don't think badly of me for that?'

'I think very well of you, Meg. Grace has told me about how it was for you. And she told me about Rex Donaldson too.'

'Oh no! Him!' she exclaimed.

Rory laughed. 'I see what you think of him now. I knew Rex a little—just the type to let women down. I'm sorry. But you're well away from him.'

'Aye, that's what I think.' Meg felt a glow of pleasure at the way he had paid her a compliment—I think very well of you, he'd said.

But her pleasure was short-lived, as he said, 'Well, Meg, give my regards to your father, and tell him I'll be calling next week. I must get back to Mother. And that charming dentist you've got in Brathay these days. She's just been invited to lunch, I believe.'

'Goodbye, then.' Meg paused, and Rory waited as he saw she had something to say. 'You'll not change Dad's medicines without a very good reason, Rory? He's set in his ways, and it would be a great pity to upset him when we know there's—nothing that can be done for him.'

Rory's voice was deep, and he touched her shoulder for a second as he said, 'I'm not that kind of doctor, Meg. I wouldn't keep good treatment to those who need it. But when nothing can help—I'll make sure he's content, trust me.' He half turned away, then added very quietly, 'You do know it—won't be long now? If the diagnosis is right.'

'Yes.' And because she felt tears coming, and wanted to throw herself into his arms, she said, 'Goodbye, then,' and ran out of the gate and into the main street, where she set her steps towards the village. He had chatted to her after all. But if she had been alone, and not with Grace, she had a strong feeling that Rory Henderson would have had little to say to wee Meg Mackenzie in her blue sprigged cotton.

She didn't look back at the kirk, but strode out towards Laurel Villa, her steps lighter because of the sunshine, and because Rory had promised that Dad wouldn't suffer. And fancy Rory knowing Rex Donaldson! She had been in love with the dashing SHO when she worked at Ninewells, and she had thought he felt the same. But he had been lighthearted about explaining his ambitions—about the fact that he collected pretty nurses as a hobby, but would never marry one. It was the way he had said it: 'You're the very best-looking, Meg. But don't forget, I'm not the settling down type, so don't be surprised if you see me with someone else. My policy is safety in numbers!' And he had expected her to laugh. Yet it was only a week later that she had seen him in a corner with a lady houseman, and their arms had been locked about each other . . . She had not been in next time Rex telephoned.

Her reflections about the past had brought her almost to the gate of Laurel Villa. The staid family home, where she had been happy while her mother was there and her father was away with the Army. But her mother had grown old and tired before her time, and she had seen her die—not from illness, but from weariness of living. Meg didn't hate her father—he couldn't help how he was made, any more than her mother could help being a martyr. Meg could even understand how her mother had been content to be dominated in the early stages of the relationship—when the man was young and handsome, and was in love, and happy to show it . . .

But Meg was an only child, so the love hadn't lasted. The bullying had. And Lily Scroggie had kept herself in the background, so that she had become invaluable to Frank when he was left with a teenage daughter to care for.

She walked up the path, neatly edged with marigolds. The lawn was trimmed and the box hedge neat. Meg felt a shiver of sadness at the lack of warmth in the grey stone house—so different from Craigie House, though made of the same granite blocks, overlooking the same sparkling sea. She rang the jangling front bell.

She was treated as a guest at Laurel Villa; that was the way her father liked it. Lily Scroggie, draped as always in a spotless white apron, opened the door to her, though she did have her own key in case of emergencies. 'Come away in, Meg. How are you keeping?'

'Fine, thank you, Mrs Scroggie.' Meg went into the lounge, where her father lay with his feet up on the couch, the Sunday paper untidy on the floor beside him, and a pack of playing cards also knocked to the floor. 'Hello, Father. You look well.'

She kissed his forehead. He asked stiffly, 'The kirk was full the day?'

'Aye, it was. How did you know?'

It was Lily who answered. 'The new doctor, like as not—young Rory Henderson, back from Africa. Dr Gregory told us he'd be calling.' She went to the great Victorian sideboard. 'You'll take a sherry, Meg?'

'Yes, please.' It was always the same—a small glass of dry sherry, and then Lily would go to see to the brisket, while father and daughter made small talk.

Major Mackenzie shifted his leg, the one with the war wound, and coughed. He thought it was chronic bronchitis that made him chair-ridden now. He said, 'You've seen Henderson?'

'Yes—he came to see Auntie Grace.' And Meg passed on the message about the raspberries.

'He came here—good-looking fellow. We talked about Africa. I've not been there, but I've seen more of India than he has. I well remember . . .'

Meg listened politely as a visitor ought. That way they got on. She looked sadly at his pale face, the yellowing bristly moustache. There was a time when he had been handsome, with the dark good looks that she had inherited, and an air of authority and stability. Now his collar was painfully large for him, his neck stringy and his breathing difficult. It was hard to be dispassionate. She ought to be here looking after him. But Lily did well, and Meg would have upset him—maybe even upset his conscience a little.

After lunch, they had chatted a little, and watched a television programme about antiques that Lily liked. Then she had made a pot of tea, served in the best china, reminding Meg that she was a guest in her own family home. And then Meg was expected to take her leave, and certainly not to offer to help in the kitchen. The sun was hidden behind a bank of cloud as she left. It didn't hurt, leaving Laurel Villa; it was just a house now, not a home. She waved to Lily and turned her face back to the south, and to Craigie House.

The rain started when she was halfway home. She was used to the Fife rain, accompanied as usual by a sudden biting wind as the tide turned, then drove the drops into her face, making her cheeks rosy and her eyes moist. She heard a car behind her, but didn't turn to look, until she recognised that cracked little hoot on the horn. Jessie Peebles drew up in her battered old Land Rover. 'Hi, Meg. You're getting wet, woman—hop in.'

'Thanks, Jess. Working today?' asked Meg.

'Well, I dinna wear a blue frock for fun.' Jessie's dimples were a blessed antidote to the stiff propriety of her recent lunch. 'I've had to go up to Nethergate Grange to give Biddy Crawfurd her injection. She hasna long to go, bless her, but she's always that grateful that it's a pleasure to go there.'

The Land Rover coughed, and juddered. Meg remarked, 'You must do some mileage in this.'

'Aye. I'm getting a new car in the new year.' Jessie pulled out the choke, and the car limped forwards. 'How's that father of yours?'

'Managing.'

'Still cheerful?'

'As cheerful as he's ever been.' Meg smiled ruefully.

'You must have been a late baby,' observed Jessie.

'I was. How did you find him?'

'Surprisingly well, considering what's wrong with him. Did you notice him wandering a bit in his speech? But dinna you fret. It will be a pleasure to look after the old warhorse.'

'Jessie, you always find something nice to say!' laughed Meg.

At Craigie House, the afternoon bridge game was over and Flora, Grace and Caroline Forbes sat over a teapot and a diminished plate of shortbread. Meg let herself in quietly and stood for a moment in the hallway, listening to the cheerful chatter of voices. There was a sudden roar of engines outside the door—motorbikes.

The Scarlet Flamingo was attracting them already, then. She tried not to think how much things had changed since the happy days of her childhood. But she was content. Craigie House was home, and she had come home.

Catriona came into the hall with a rush. 'I thought I heard the door, Meg. Will I get you another cuppie of tea?'

'No, thanks, Caddy.' Catriona was a plump and not very attractive youngster. Yet such a talented cook, such a sweet nature. Too young to be hiding away. Even those rowdy bike boys would be only Caddy's age. 'You never take much time off, Caddy,' Meg added.

'I like it here,' Catriona smiled.

'All work and no play. You sound like Jessie Peebles!'

'Folk are different. Anyway, this is play. I've got my television and my books.' Catriona showed a romantic novel with a highly coloured woman on the front with very few clothes on. Meg smiled. What did Caddy really know of life? The girl went back to her cosy kitchen and her television set.

'Hello, Meg Mackenzie.' Meg jumped. She hadn't realised there was anyone in the library. Rory smiled. 'I've been browsing—there are some damn good books in there. Auntie ought to sell.'

'Why should she? We read quite a lot, specially about music, and great composers.' She remembered something. 'You used to play the piano too—I remember your lesson was after mine on a Friday. Are you any good?'

'Good? I'm bloody marvellous!'

Suddenly she laughed aloud, no longer afraid of him. That was the secret. 'I see. There's nothing like confidence.'

'The sooner you believe that, Meg, the easier life becomes,' he assured her.

'I'll try and remember that.' They walked together into the drawing room, where Caddy followed them to put down the card table and take away the tea tray.

Rory said, grinning, 'We've come for our music lesson, Auntie.'

Grace clapped her hands together. 'Oh, how well I remember!' The useless hand lay on her knee, as she clapped the other upon it. 'You, the great tall schoolboy, and that wee child who was just away as you arrived.'

Caroline, in her cut glass accent, said, 'How terribly sweet.'

Flora began to feel left out. 'Rory, we should be on our way——' she began.

'Sure, Mother, I'll take you home.'

Caroline stood up. 'I'll be off too, Miss Henderson. Thank you again for a delightful day.'

Rory followed Caroline out. Meg was by the open door, and heard him say, 'Seven tonight, then?'

And Caroline's reply, 'I'm looking forward to it.'

Rory said, 'Folk tend to talk around here.'

'So I've noticed. So what?' Caroline laughed.

'See you,' he said.

And Meg wished she hadn't heard it.

The sound of Rory's car faded into the distance, and suddenly all they could hear was the distant roar of the ocean. Grace was lying on the sofa, a tartan rug round her legs. 'That was very pleasant. I'm lucky to have the company of young people.'

They sat down for a while, Caddy joining them as usual. 'What would you like for your supper, Miss Henderson?' she asked.

'Have we a kipper? You feel like a kipper, Meg?'

Catriona said, 'I always have smokies in.'

'Of course. Arbroath smokies, then, with brown rolls, butter and a little watercress.' They ate supper on trays, watching television. Meg tried not to look at the clock, knowing that she was waiting to hear the engine of the scarlet car as Rory kept his assignation with Caroline. The grandfather clock in the hall struck seven. She could

hear the ticking as the minutes passed without anyone
passing on the road.

Then she heard it, at first like the growl of some far-
off lion, then getting closer, closer . . . and it stopped
at the door of Craigie House. She jumped up without thinking, and Grace said drily, 'You expecting
anyone?'

Meg realised she had been a little too eager. Casually
she said, 'Surely you recognise Rory's car? He must have
forgotten something.' She went to the door, opening it
almost before he rang the bell.

'Hi, Meg. Can I borrow a couple of books?'

Grace called from the drawing room, 'Of course you
can. But don't lose them, and let me know which ones
you choose.'

Meg went with him into the library. It was still light,
but she put on the small reading lamp to give him extra
help. He went to the window first. 'The tide is high
tonight,' he observed. She waited for him to confess
where he was going, but he just turned and took a couple
of calf-bound history books. 'Thanks.' He put the light
off and went in to show Grace what he had borrowed,
and kissed her before going to the door.

Meg waited at the door, remembering his touch, that
first day. He paused but didn't touch her. 'This is a
strange time of day, you know, Meg. We don't have
dusk in Africa. The times I've sat in a tent, slapping at
the flies as the sun went down with a rush across the
scrublands. And I've thought of Brathay, with its gentle
rains and luminous waters . . .'

'I've never wanted to go far away.' She looked up
boldly. 'But of course you would know that—small-
town girl that I am . . .'

'I never meant to offend you,' he said hastily.

'You didn't care whether you did or not.'

'Is that what you think?'

She said shortly, 'It doesn't matter what I think.
You'd best be on your way. Punctuality is a sign of a

gentleman.' As she spoke the grandfather clock struck the quarter.

Rory didn't move. Instead he turned right round to face her, and he was smiling suddenly. 'You know, Meg, Rex Donaldson must have been out of his mind.' He took a firmer grip on the books in his hand and ran down the steps without looking back. Meg watched him briefly, then closed the door, wondering why he had suddenly paid her a compliment. She had said nothing particularly clever. That was Caroline's talent: Meg had only spoken her mind. She shook her head. Men were peculiar. But one compliment wasn't going to make her join the ranks of his admirers. Meg Mackenzie was tougher than that.

All the same, as Meg washed Grace and prepared her for bed that evening, she found her mind alive in a most unusual way. There was something vibrant and exciting in her suddenly. She was as gentle as always with Grace, as she buttoned up the soft cotton nightdress and smoothed the pillows, but Grace noticed. 'There's a faraway look in your eyes, lassie,' she said. 'I'd understand if it were spring, now. But autumn is coming, a strange time to get restless.'

Meg had always talked very frankly to Grace, but tonight she couldn't even explain her feelings to herself, so she just said, 'No, I'm not restless, just not ready for bed yet.'

Grace said innocently, 'Did Rory say anything to you?'

'Nothing important.' She tucked in the bedclothes. 'You must be happy to have him back.'

'I am, dear. God bless, Meg.'

'God bless, Auntie.' Meg put out the bedside lamp and went through to her own room. It was too early to sleep. She went down to the kitchen, where Catriona was sitting, eyes closed, tapping her feet to the pulsating rhythms of some modern group. She jumped up when Meg came in.

'Don't disturb yourself.' Meg sat down at the kitchen table, scrubbed spotless as usual. 'Why do you never go out, Caddy? Don't you even want to see your mum and dad?' Dad was on the buses, Mum cleaned for a couple of local shops.

'A bit. But the house is always untidy. I like it here.'

'If you like music, you should go up to Jimmy Stewart's some time. Don't your friends ever go there?'

'Aye, they do,' answered Catriona.

'Then come on, Caddy, let's go and have a coffee down there. The evening's too nice to stay in.'

'Honest?' Caddy's eyes were round. 'You really want to go?'

'Sure. Jimmy's almost an uncle. I've been there since I started school, haven't you, Caddy?'

'Och aye, after school. But not these days.'

'Come away, then,' smiled Meg. 'I'll buy you a cappuccino.'

'Och, thanks!' Catriona was as excited as though Meg had offered to take her to the Old Course Hotel in St Andrews—a grand edifice that Meg had not yet dared to enter. The two girls walked down the road, the afterglow of the sunset beautiful in the sky, and Meg despised herself a little for making use of Catriona, when she realised she wanted to go to Jimmy's in order to pass Blackrock View, the small but impeccably stylish bungalow belonging to Caroline Frobes.

They had a coffee, and listened to the jukebox music, watched the teenagers from a corner table, and the black-leathered motorbikers acting big in their boots and helmets, but underneath quite ordinary lads. Caddy actually met a couple of girls she had been to school with, and chatted with them happily while Meg talked to Jimmy.

The scarlet car was still discreetly parked at the side of the bungalow as they walked home at midnight. Meg was unusually quiet, though Catriona chattered, the evening having stimulated her to take up a more normal

life for a teenager. She went to bed immediately, and
Meg had a bath before standing at her window in the
dark, staring down the road. 'Go home, Rory Henderson. Go home, for the love of good sense.' But the road
was quiet.

The bikers began to roar past at about two in the
morning. Meg began to feel sleepy, and pulled her
housecoat closer round her as even Jimmy's customers
went home, and the coast road was left to the eternal
washing of the sea, murmuring and growling as far as she
could see to the horizon and past it. The moon was
hidden now by ragged clouds, occasionally showing
through briefly, sending a jagged silver pathway almost
to the gates of Craigie House.

She gave up then, and went to bed. Sleep finally came
to her, as she appreciated the soft pillow, the comfortable bed. And then, perversely, as though waiting for
her to sleep, came the gentle roar of a red sports car,
nosing out of Blackrock View and driving slowly
through the village, as though trying not to disturb the
neighbours. Meg stirred and turned over, hearing the
noise but not identifying it. The grandfather clock in
the hall chimed three o'clock.

CHAPTER THREE

FOR A FEW days life went on as routinely as though the village hadn't been invaded by Rory Henderson. Meg cared for Grace lovingly, Catriona cooked for them, they went for walks together, shopped, and watched television. On Saturday Meg played squash, and went to Laurel Villa for supper afterwards. Her father was sleepy and had little to say, and Mrs Scroggie didn't encourage her to stay. She went home early, and as always, she was happy to get back to Craigie House.

'Thank goodness to be home!' She brushed Grace's hair, pure white after it had been washed.

'You've come from one invalid to another, lass. How was your father?'

'Content, but sleepy.' Meg put the brush back and pushed the wheelchair over so that Grace could slide into bed. 'I never think of you as an invalid, Auntie. Even though you're weakly, your mind isn't. It's like with someone of my own age—except with a bit more wisdom, I suppose.'

Grace settled herself on the pillow. 'Flora and Rory will be coming as usual—I telephoned while you were out.'

'And Caroline?'

Grace smiled. 'And Caroline. I know she sees lots of patients during the day, but she still lives alone, Meg, and that can be sad, at her age.'

'I bet it can.' Meg bit back the remark, as she envisaged that sleek red car in its usual parking place along the side of Blackrock View. 'I'm sure it can.'

Sunday passed as it had last week, with the exception that Rory Henderson did not make an opportunity to chat to Meg alone. He was more concerned with his work now, as he saw more patients, and became immersed in general practice. As he left with Flora, he said, 'I'll be hoping to see you at the Argyle Hall on Wednesday.'

Meg was seeing them out. 'You know we never miss anything on there.'

Flora agreed. 'Grace and I have been benefactors over the years—she paid for the new guttering, as I recall, and I contributed to the organ overhaul.' She looked up at Meg. 'And you gave us some very nice lessons on first aid last year.'

Meg smiled. 'I enjoyed it. But the Boy Scouts who had to be covered with tomato sauce to be patients enjoyed it even more!'

Rory said, 'I hope my slides aren't a bit too realistic for the village.'

Meg was quick to retort. 'Oh no. Even small-town people have consciences, Rory, don't fret. They've seen famine on their televisions, you know.'

Rory turned to help his mother down the last step. He looked back with a grimace. 'I'll never live that down, will I, Meg?'

'Time will tell,' she answered tartly. 'Good night to you both.'

There was no need to be early on Wednesday at the hall, because Mr Moncreiff always saved Meg a seat on the end of the front row, where Grace's wheelchair could be placed beside her. They came in to find the entrance hall crowded as usual, Mr Moncreiff in his dinner suit greeting everyone as he stood beside the programme of coming events, from Weight-Watchers to the course in disco-dancing run by Miss Wylie who used to dance on television.

Rory came out of the hall, where he had been supervising the projector that was to show his slides. He nodded to Mr Moncreiff. 'Ready.' He was relaxed and casual in a tweed jacket over an open-necked shirt, but his height and his good looks made him the most striking figure there. He noticed Grace at that moment, and gave them a wide smile as he said, 'My guests of honour are here, Moncreiff. We can start now.'

Meg thought again that if she had been alone, without Grace Henderson, Rory would scarcely have noticed wee Meg Mackenzie. She pushed the chair into the crowded hall, and Grace was greeted on all sides. As they took their places, Rory and Mr Moncreiff walked up to the platform, and the murmuring of voices gradually ceased. Rory's eyes, such a clear true blue, captured the audience without any need of gimmicks. He just came to the front of the stage and spoke.

The lights dimmed then, and there was a spontaneous burst of applause, as though the village wanted to show Rory that he was welcomed home by all of them. He thanked them modestly for remembering him. He said a few words about the changes in Brathay, including a mention of the Scarlet Flamingo, which got a chuckle, and a reference to the old minister, whom he had crossed more than once with his boyish pranks. He praised the new minister warmly, and Alistair had to stand up from his place at the front and acknowledge the compliments with a nod of thanks.

Then Rory started to tell the story of the raw young doctor arriving newly in Jibuti, before the long trek by lorry to the famine areas. The audience was putty in his hands. He spoke well, vividly describing his own feelings. Meg could understand how he felt. Even after five years at university, he was not prepared for such sights of deprivation and misery, trained as he was in modern medicine, with full hospital back-up.

'Now we'll show you some pictures. Some are sad, some are heartrending, but many are encouraging and hopeful. And I know that this one evening in this little town will be an extra grain of encouragement for those I have left there still caring and still hoping.'

He was right. When the lights went on again, and coffee was served, the collecting boxes clinked satisfyingly with pound coins, and rustled nicely with paper money. Alistair had made the closing vote of thanks. Now he was moving amongst the collectors, thanking the givers warmly. Caroline Forbes asked for him to turn round, so that she could write a cheque with the help of his shoulders to lean her cheque book on. She was wearing elegant black, and made sure that the people around them knew that the cheque was for three figures. Meg and Grace exchanged a smile, as they quietly added their own not inconsiderable contributions to the box.

Rory was by now besieged with people wanting to hear more about how they could help. Some wanted to tell him their own travel stories. And some just wanted to shake him by the hand and welcome him home after his long absence, and hope that he wouldn't be going away again. Caroline had somehow wormed her way to his side, and her pretty laugh echoed across the room as Meg helped Grace with her coffee cup, and handed fairy cakes to Miss MacFarlane.

The schoolmistress said, 'You used to play with Rory, as I recall, Meg.'

Meg laughed. 'Not exactly play. Hamish and Marian and our little gang used to pester Rory's group to take us with them. Sometimes he put up with us, but I can still hear his voice now as he shouted at us to get away home, and not bother the big boys.'

Miss MacFarlane shook her head. 'Och well, he'll not be doing that these days, I'm sure of that.'

'In his own way, I think he is,' smiled Meg. 'I think I'm still wee Meg to him, even now.'

'Then I hope he realises that it's quality, not quantity, that matters.' Miss MacFarlane was sharp, but only because years of teaching had instilled that way of speaking in her.

Grace pulled Meg's arm, and she bent to hear her say, 'Meg dear, sorry to rush you, but it's my bladder again.'

This was a normal problem, and Meg was quite used

to making excuses and getting them both out of company with the minimum of fuss. 'No problem, Auntie.' She was glad to get away herself, to be honest, away from the claustrophobic atmosphere and the sight of Rory and Caroline as the centre of the village's attention. They slipped out of the side door, as the laughter and chatter went on with no signs of abatement.

Meg settled Grace for the night. It was work, and she was paid for it, but she was fond of the old lady, and did it willingly, for Grace was more of a parent to her than her father. She knew that subconsciously she took the place of the mother she had lost. 'I'll just take a wee walk, Auntie, but I'll be back by eleven. Have you got the bell string close by?'

'Yes, dear.' Grace looked very tiny as she cuddled into the pillow. 'You never tire, do you, lass?'

'I expect you were just the same at my age,' said Meg gently.

'I expect I was, but it seems so long ago that I must have forgotten.'

Meg put out the light, knowing where she was going. After the talk tonight of the old days, she was going down to the flat rock on the beach below the house, the rock where as children they used to congregate, to share out their booty, whether it be wild strawberries, cockles, or just pink shells or pebbles they thought might be precious stones. And the sound of the sea would soothe her, as it always did, and drive away her jealousy of Caroline Forbes, with her bewitching smile and total self-confidence.

She could hear above the waves the sound of cars and distant voices, as the Argyle Hall gave up its occupants. She could also hear the roar of bikes, as the younger generation proved their manhood by making a loud noise and dressing in black. It was far enough away not to wake Grace. She wondered how many of them even spared a thought for the refugees of the Sudan. Did they ever think what it felt like to have no notion of where the next meal would be coming from—or even if one would come at all . . .

She shivered suddenly, though she had put a thick sweater on over her dress. Perhaps it was time to go back. The gentle waters had done their work, stilling her troubled thoughts, and reminding her of the permanent beauty that surrounded her. She had been sitting on the flat rock, the toes of her shoes in the sand. Now she stood up and stretched her back and shoulders. She heard the crunch of pebbles, and a low voice said, 'Is it yourself, Meg Mackenzie?'

She knew who it was without turning. But she did turn, a sudden lift in her heart. 'Rory Henderson—I thought you'd be still with your admirers.'

He had just taken a step off the road on to the beach. Now he strolled across the sand slowly towards her, his hands deep in his pockets. He stopped, looked out to sea, and gave a deep sigh—of contentment more than sorrow. 'I'd forgotten this beach. We used to use this rock for sharing things out. And Auntie Grace would be teaching the piano, and the sound would come down to us, and when the last pupil left we'd know there was lemonade if we called.'

Meg said nothing. She too had half forgotten that, but at his words she could almost hear the halting notes as some child who had not done his practice would struggle with a chromatic scale, or hammer out 'The Merry Peasant' with more gusto than finesse. She said almost to herself, 'It always seemed to be summer.'

They stood together, slightly selfconscious at meeting unexpectedly, as though they both had private feelings they didn't want the other to know about. After a while Meg said, 'You did well tonight. Raised a good sum for the refugees.'

'We did—a small drop in the ocean of need, but generous beyond my expectations.' Rory went on with a faintly mocking tone, 'I see you didn't wait to congratulate me, Meg.'

She smiled in the darkness. 'No need. You had quite a fan club!' And she knew he recognised her veiled reference to Caroline. She sat down again on the rock. 'You always used to be able to find cockles.'

'It was easy. You had to look for the tiny blowhole in the wet sand.'

They were both beset by memories. Memories of carefree children roving this cove, discovering the sheltered crannies among the rocks, where they could sit in a private huddle, sharing the wild things they had collected for their feasts. This time of year was best, for there were hazelnuts and berries, fennel and sweet ears of corn.

Rory said, looking out to sea, 'So how do you think I've made out as the new country GP?'

Meg smiled. 'You want me to do your audience research?'

'You're more observant than some.'

'Thank you. But I might be honest.'

'I only want the truth,' he assured her.

'Well, you're a wonderful doctor, but a little too keen. You want to cure everyone—even those who've only come along for a chat.'

'I'm a doctor, not a social worker.'

'You still don't see that telling you their troubles is a cure in itself. Telling someone who understands.'

'I thought that was Alistair Reid's job.'

'Yours too.' Meg looked up at the square shoulders, the back of the dark head, just visible against the vague glow where the moon should have been. A curlew cried out over the bay—a sad sound, though the wild creature was probably enjoying its wheeling flight. Meg said, 'Will you stay with us in Brathay?'

'No. I could never settle. I must be up and doing, where I feel I can do more than just chat.'

Disappointed, she said, 'You'll be studying for your Membership exams, then?'

'Aye. I've bought the books. Lucky you're a healthy

lot in Brathay—I've found time to start my studies.'

'And after that?'

'Anywhere. I've applied to Aberdeen, Leeds and Birmingham so far.'

Meg said to his still turned back, 'They have the same germs as Brathay.'

He turned to face her then, and she could see the white of his teeth as he smiled in the darkness. 'Aye, they do, Meg. And they don't have the sharing-rock, and the wild sea and the kirk and Auntie Grace—and they don't have Meg Mackenzie either. But I live in the real world, Meg, and I've made my plans. I'll get nowhere here.'

She said quietly, 'Then good luck, Rory.'

'You mean that, don't you?'

'I do. I always say what I mean.'

He nodded. 'Aye.' There was a long silence between them, no longer embarrassing or selfconscious, just neighbourly. Then Rory said, 'I'll be calling on your father Monday, Meg. About twelve, if you want to be there.'

'Thanks.'

She watched him stride up the rocks, crunch across the gravel to the road. He was very agile, slim—the life in Africa had not been one to encourage putting on weight. And she began to realise that she wasn't antagonistic to him any more. As she had got to know him again, she recognised the same sincerity in him that led him to speak the truth to her, whether it be flattering or not —just as she had told him tonight to his face that he was over-zealous as a country GP. Somehow, tonight had sealed them as friends. It was all she could expect, and she was glad of it.

Her father wanted to talk a lot, when she next called at Laurel Villa. She was heartened by the animation in him, so different from the last few visits. He reminisced about some of the family holidays they'd had—some that she scarcely remembered, but he did, and with some affection for her mother too . . .

'You still playing squash, Meg?'

'Yes—I'm in the team, you know.'

'I never saw squash as a woman's game,' he remarked.

'There isn't much these days that women don't do.'

He leaned back against the cushions, gasping for breath. Meg didn't make him talk, but as soon as he could, he started again. 'Jessie Peebles is a good woman.'

'One of the best,' she agreed.

'I'd like you to give her something when I'm gone, Meg. A picture, maybe, or an ornament—something valuable.'

Meg's heart was touched. 'I'll do that. But no need to talk about it now.'

'There's some jewellery too. You'd better take it, it's yours.'

'But——'

'Take it, lass—it's yours. You know where the safe key is.' The effort of raising his voice made him cough. Meg obeyed him, and opened the safe in the corner. Inside were two boxes, one with a pair of magnificent diamond earrings and one with a string of pearls. They had been her mother's; Meg remembered her wearing them, looking pretty and happy . . . she carried the boxes over to him. He said, 'They're yours now. Don't forget to insure them.'

'Thank you. I'll treasure them.'

'I've written a few things down—for when I'm gone. Young Reid is the other executor.'

'Father—' Meg tried to hold back tears, 'You were always good at organising things. But you don't need to tell me all this yet.'

'Army training. It never leaves you, you know. Better than I tell you now, and then there's no misunderstanding.'

And as she walked home, carrying her precious cargo in a brown paper bag, she wondered if Frank Mackenzie was right in thinking he was going to die. Yet such was his authority that she knew it would irritate and upset him if she went back, begged to be allowed to stay with him. She plodded on, hating the distance between them, but knowing that there was nothing else to be done. That night, she didn't sleep.

Subconsciously next day she knew she was waiting for the telephone to ring, because she hovered about close to it for most of the morning. And when the first shrill notes began, she had the receiver to her ear at once. 'Lily?'

'How did you ken it was me?'

'I know he wasn't feeling well yesterday, Lily. How is he?'

'In hospital. I called the doctor, and he examined him and sent him into Ninewells.'

'Why, Lily—oh, why? Wouldn't it have been kinder to leave him at home?'

The woman agreed. 'Aye. But Dr Henderson wasna convinced that he'd get all the treatment he needed here. Maybe you'd better speak to the hospital yourself, Meg, because I dinna believe they can work miracles.'

'Have you phoned the hospital yourself?' Meg asked.

'Of course. They said he's being prepared for theatre. It was one of them snooty Sisters. She said the surgeon believed his condition was curable, Meg. Do you believe that, Meg—you saw him yesterday?'

Meg's heart beat painfully with a sudden surge of hope. Frank Mackenzie was a cussed old soul, but he was her father, and they had some happy memories in common. 'I'll phone, Lily. They wouldn't operate if they didn't think it would help. I'll ring when I find out anything.' Either Rory Henderson had interfered—or he had miraculously done the right thing in the nick of time. She tried not to raise her hopes too high. Rory was young and possibly impulsive. But on the other hand, an experienced surgeon had thought it worthwhile to operate . . .

She ran to tell Grace the news. 'Do you think—I ought to be with him?' she asked anxiously.'

Grace nodded at once. 'No need to ask, dear. Away you go, and please God there is still a lot of hope.'

Meg paused at the door. 'I wonder? I wonder if it was right to do this, or whether poor Father will pass away surrounded by white walls and tubes and strangers. What peace or dignity will he have now?'

Grace said in her familiar sharp way, 'There's no finding out without going to see for yourself. We won't start blaming anyone yet.'

Meg nodded, and turned, pulling on her coat. 'You love that nephew of yours. To you he can do no wrong, eh, Auntie? Och well, by tonight we'll all know the truth.'

'Aye. God be with you both.'

Grace's words echoed in her ears, as she set out on a still grey day to drive the twenty miles north across the countryside and the grey misty river. The silvery Tay, they called it, but it was glum and unsparkling today. She drove through the grey streets of Dundee, and out on to the Perth road, where she had once lived as a student nurse. But there was no time for memories now. She parked quickly in the modern car park and ran to the front door of the gleaming hospital and up the stairs to the ward Lily had mentioned.

'Miss Mackenzie?' Sister was new to her, bright-eyed, middle aged and tiny, reminding her of a sparrow. 'Come away in. Your father is out of surgery, but still in Intensive Care. I'll have a word for you, and maybe you can go and see him in a moment. Sit down for a wee while—the coffee trolley is on its way.'

Meg held her cup and saucer, held it stiffly like a trophy, her muscles tense with worry as Sister spoke on the phone. She heard scraps of the conversation— breathing difficulties, poor pulse, left ventricular failure . . . Meg began to wish with all her heart that Rory Henderson had stayed out of her life.

Sister put down the phone. 'Holding his own, dear. The surgeon is with him, and he'll be down in a few minutes to have a word.'

'Which surgeon is it?' Meg asked.

'Mr Donaldson. One of our top men, Miss Mac-kenzie.'

'Donaldson!' Meg felt as though she had been thumped in the stomach. The coffee cup teetered in her hand. Rex Donaldson was the one man in Ninewells she never wanted to see again. The man who had treated her as he treated all the nurses, blandishing her when he felt like it, and throwing her over when a prettier one came along. Her heart beat painfully fast. If only the house-man could bring news of her father—she didn't want to speak to the top man, not to Rex Donaldson, even though she had long ago ceased to care twopence for him.

Meg forced herself to turn and walk to a window, where she stood, sipping the cold coffee, every nerve jangling as she waited. Rex Donaldson operating on her father! She felt warm at memories of his honeyed words, his twinkling, deceiving eyes, his dark crinkly hair and dark smooth voice . . .

'Meg Mackenzie? *The* Meg Mackenzie?'

Yes, it was Rex. No other surgeon would have known her first name. Rex Donaldson had good reason to—he had said it so gently, making it sound like the loveliest name in the world. She turned slowly. Whatever news was coming, the meeting was bound to be painful. 'Yes?'

They faced each other. Rex was still in theatre green, mask pulled down, curls half hidden by the unbecoming cap. His eyes were as devastating as ever, and he held out his hand warmly. Meg put down the cup. and allowed her cold hand to be shaken. 'Meg dear, how are you? As lovely as ever, I see, if not lovelier.' He held up a hand to prevent her question. 'Your father first, of course. He's a lucky man, Meg—must have a superb GP. He's something else. When all the signs pointed to cancer, he decided just in time—just in time, Meg—that the neoplasm could be benign. And it was, Meg. Histology did an urgent check for me before I closed, in case I had to do more radical surgery. There's no cancer in that man, and after a couple of days when he'll feel uncomfortable, he'll be as good as new. Not that I'll be permitting a three-minute mile—not with one and a half lungs. But he'll live, Meg, and he won't die of this problem. We've taken it away, and all he needs now is rest.'

'Oh, Rex!' Meg felt an enormous wave of relief. She felt her head begin to spin, and she groped for a chair. Rex was quick to support her, to snap his fingers for a glass of water to be brought. 'Thank you!'

'Steady on! Don't try to say anything. Anyway, it wasn't a difficult operation. It's your family doctor you must thank. If he hadn't got him here, the swelling would have blocked the bronchus and he might have choked to death. Who is he, by the way? New chap?'

'Rory Henderson. He's from Brathay, but been in the Sudan for a while.'

'I remember the name,' said Rex. 'Well, there's one gentleman who's on the ball. Now, are there any questions? Like when can I see you again?'

She couldn't help smiling with relief. 'Keep the conversation to Father, please. When can I see him?'

'If you're extra nice to me, I can fix it for you to pop your head into ICU, just for a minute. You've seen surgical cases, you know it'll be twenty-four hours before he picks up.'

Frank Mackenzie was almost unrecognisable under an oxygen mask, with catheter, drip, and antibiotic cover. But as Meg neared the bed she saw that his pale blue eyes were open. She touched his hand. 'Do you know where you are, Father?' she asked softly.

His voice was muffled, but she could hear him through the mask. 'In hospital, of course. Where else would they wrap me up like a Christmas parcel?' He shivered suddenly, and the hovering nurse ran to tuck him in.

Meg said, 'It will be post-operative chill. I'll just sit here, if I may, for a few minutes. It's so wonderful to see him like this, pink with the transfused blood, instead of yellow like last night.'

And to her surprise, Frank joined in the conversation. 'Young Henderson knew what to do, Meg. Wouldn't listen to my objections—and quite right too.' The effort of speaking made him gasp, but after a couple of breaths of oxygen, he was again tranquilly resting.

Meg looked down at the blood seeping into the drainage bottle. 'Well, you won't be too comfortable for a day or so, Father—but after that, you'll soon be home, and better than new.'

She saw his eyes crinkle into a smile. 'That's the trouble with having a nurse as a daughter—no coddling now! She'll keep telling me there's nothing wrong.'

Meg and the other nurse joined in his laughter. But Meg said, 'I'd better let you rest now. Lily and I will be in to see you tomorrow. Be good!'

'Right, lass.' And as Meg turned at the door to give him a little wave, she heard him say, 'And my thanks to young Henderson. Tell him I'm grateful.'

When she got home, Alistair was there with Grace and Catriona, and they shared a quiet supper, after Meg had phoned Lily Scroggie and given her the glad news. Alistair talked happily about miracles, declaring himself a specialist on the subject. After a while Meg excused herself. She knew she had to go to Rory; she could not rest that night if she did not see him to thank him in person.

The moon was just coming up in a dark blue sky, luminous at the horizon. The sea whispered tonight, whispered of miracles, of human skill and of the spirit of joy that hung over the entire village. They shared in the joys as well as the sorrows of their neighbours, and the relief over her father's recovery felt by the whole village was tangible tonight.

Rory had been here more than two months now, accepted as though he had never been away. 'Whoops —steady on! Oh, Meg, it's you.' It was Rory himself, who had been walking up Harbour Lane as fast as she had been walking down it. 'Where are you off to at this time of night?'

She looked up at him in the moonlight. 'Where else, Rory Henderson? Here to see you, to confess that I was wrong—that I had no right to tell you your job—that you're a brilliant family doctor, and that I know now that you have a skill, a sixth sense that can spot something wrong even against all the evidence. You are——'

'I'll accept your apology gracefully, lass. You don't have to make a speech.' There was amusement and affection in his voice.

Meg responded in the same vein. 'I'm a small-town girl, Rory. I maybe get things wrong sometimes.'

'None of that, lass. Everyone gets things wrong. And you were right when you begged me not to interfere with nature. I agree with you—one hundred per cent. Honestly. Especially when the X-rays definitely showed a lung lesion.' He reached out in the darkness and patted her shoulder. 'Only you have to know that my rule is to always go on looking, just in case. I guess my motto has to be where there's life there's hope. I truly mean that. And on the few occasions when it works, no one is happier than I.'

'Except the families you save from despair.'

'Shall I walk you back, Meg?' Rory asked.

'No need.' But she was glad when he turned her gently and walked with her. 'It's just that I couldn't rest until I'd told you how happy Father and I are,'she explained. 'Even covered with tubes and masks and drips, he couldn't hide his happiness, Rory. He must have been living with the fear of cancer—his weight loss was just through depression. You spotted it, Rory—and it's almost like being raised from the dead.' Tears filled her eyes, as they both walked slowly up the brae.

At the gate they paused. He said, 'I will not come in—Grace's bedtime.'

Meg had been weeping silently. Suddenly she turned and threw her arms round his neck and hugged him hard. Taken aback, he stumbled, but soon steadied himself and caught her against him, making the embrace a mutual one, his own arms even stronger than hers. He whispered into her hair, 'You're soaking my shirt, lass, but you're welcome. I was only doing my job—and it's good when it works out.'

She drew back. 'Oh, I'm sorry.'

They stood: Rory took her hands in his. 'It's been a good day.' He let go her hands. 'Meg, if I may, I'd like to come round for your advice soon—about drugs, and the local teenagers. Heroin is getting about, as well as the softer stuff, and I don't know where to turn. It's something that mustn't take hold in Brathay.' He paused. 'Someone's tried to break open my drugs cupboard.'

Meg nodded. 'I'm not going anywhere, except the hospital in the afternoons. Come when you like. I suppose Father will be in a couple of weeks?'

'Make it three—he was very weak. If I know those chaps, they'll want to be sure he's fit before they let him go home to a winter on the North Sea coast.'

Meg watched him go, her heart full of gratitude.

CHAPTER FOUR

'THAT'S three times Rory's been round for a private chat.' Grace wasn't prying, she was merely stating a fact. 'I'm glad he is realising that you are a sensible person to discuss things with.'

Meg had been glad to help Rory. She had talked over the possibility of crime coming into Brathay with the advent of Jimmy's wine bar and the consequent invasion of teenagers with nothing to do and money to spend. She had promised to keep her eyes open when she called in at Jimmy's. And Rory had been grateful for her knowledge of the place, and of the people. But she was still affected by his first impressions of her. 'It isn't that he thinks my mentality has improved, Auntie. He just wanted to talk to someone who knows Jimmy, and some of the local youngsters. I know both, with living here so long, that's all.'

Grace nodded, but didn't interfere. 'I'm glad you can help him out,' was all she said. 'Now that Dr Gregory had gone off on his annual holiday, Rory is a lot busier than he ever thought he would be in such a sleepy place.'

'Without Jessie Peebles, I think he'd be run off his feet—she's an angel. Nothing is too much trouble for Jess, whatever the weather. She mothers us all.'

'I know,' Grace agreed, 'No one could replace that woman. I wish she could get a medal or a decoration —she deserves it a lot more than some I could mention.'

'I agree. No one could replace Jessie.'

Winter was showing signs of descending on them soon, with a series of night frosts, although it was only late October. Meg set off for the surgery for Grace's monthly prescriptions, and had to go back for a thicker sweater. She wore trousers mostly. Grace's central heating was good, but the rooms in the house were high, and feet and legs got chilly with the continual wind from the east. It was Monday morning.

'Hello, Mrs Blyth.' The middle-aged woman in her tea-cosy hat and striped hand-knitted cardigan had been at Dr Gregory's since Meg was a child, and showed no signs of ageing. 'Can I just collect Auntie's repeat prescription?'

'Och, of course you can. Sit here out of the cold, Meg, and I'll get it for you.'

'Dr Henderson run off his feet yet?' asked Meg.

'Not yet, but he thinks he is. He has no idea how frantic we can be, once the snows begin.' Mrs Blyth trotted off into the consulting room. There were about four people in the waiting room, and Meg was just exchanging comments about the change in the weather, when something of a whirlwind erupted in from the lane.

'Where's that doctor? Where's Dr Henderson? I demand to see him this minute! Come away, Mrs Blyth, out of my way. That man is nothing but a monster, and I demand that he be struck off the medical register the minute before he's let loose on any other innocent girl. Get him out here, woman. You canna protect him from justice, I warn you!'

Meg put out a hand to stop her. 'Mrs Campbell, what's the matter? Who are you talking about? Just wait a minute, and catch your breath.' For indeed, the small thin woman who had swept in was breathing heavily, and her pinched-looking face was pink with anger, her eyes staring. She was usually so mild and proper, doing the flowers in the kirk, and visiting the sick.

Rory came to the door in his white coat, hearing the noise. The patient with him was just leaving. 'What is it, Mrs Campbell? An emergency?'

'It's my Morag, that's what it is, as well you ken, Dr Henderson. Dinna you emergency me, young man—and dinna be sending me to the end of the queue either! You laid hands on my daughter, you did, you assaulted her when she came to you in trust and innocence. I call on these folk to witness what this so-called doctor has done to my child!'

The others in the waiting room were wide-eyed at this outburst. Mrs Campbell was half Rory's size, but she faced him as a sparrow might face a lion to protect its young. Rory said gently, 'Come into the consulting room. Nothing wrong has happened here, I assure you.' He turned to the others. 'You didn't mind if we settle Mrs Campbell's fears first, do you?'

'I will no come into that consulting room, not after the way you treated my Morag! Covered in bruises, she was, where you mauled her—her—bosom! I will no keep quiet either. The whole town better know what our pretty new doctor does to innocent girls. A beast would not have done what you did!'

Meg tried to stop her. 'Mrs Campbell, please don't shout. There must be some misunderstanding. Why not go through and explain to the doctor and Mrs Blyth why you suddenly decided it was the doctor and not Morag's boyfriend?'

The woman rounded on her. 'A boyfriend wouldna hurt her like that. Some animal did that. And she was here for a medical the Friday night. That's when she was molested.'

Rory said loudly, his eyes steely, 'That is a complete lie, Mrs Campbell. I don't know why the child should accuse me. She came for a medical, yes, but Mrs Blyth is always present. She'll corroborate that there's no truth in the girl's accusation.'

'Of course I will!' Mrs Blyth was bristling with indignation. 'How could you! And you a God-fearing body as you are, with a respect for the truth.'

'Are you telling me you didna touch her—her—bosom?'

He looked steadily at the woman, and then at the assembled patients. 'Breast examination is a normal part of a medical examination.'

Mrs Blyth interrupted. 'You'd be annoyed if she had a lump that the doctor didn' find, I'll be bound!'

Mrs Campbell, still breathing hard, turned to the receptionist. 'And you saw it all? You were there all the time? Morag says you had to go and answer the telephone.'

'She was still in the room, Mrs Campbell.' Meg felt sorry for Rory, as he tried to be reasonable with the hysterical woman.

'But she was distracted! That's when the offence took place, and that's what my lawyer is going to hear about this afternoon.' The woman gave him a final glare, burst into tears, and swept out of the surgery.

Rory said quietly, 'Now, who's next?' and went on with seeing patients as though nothing had happened. Meg retreated with Mrs Blyth into her own little office, both women shattered by the Greek tragedy that had just been acted out in front of them.

'It isna true, Meg, it just isna true,' Mrs Blyth protested. 'She's lying, to cover up for some bruises her boyfriend must have made.'

'Surely no one will believe her,' declared Meg.

'Surely no.' The two women sat in stunned silence until Rory had finished, when he came and joined them in the office, sitting glumly on a small high stool.

Meg said, 'She's a pretty girl—lots of admirers. Why would she want to land anyone in trouble?'

Rory sighed. 'I don't think her mother knows what teenagers get up to these days. We were just saying last night, weren't we, Meg? It's no use blaming Jimmy Stewart. They'd only go somewhere else.' He straightened his shoulders, and said, 'How about some coffee, Mrs Blyth? I still don't know what they've got against me. I doubt if she'd have suspected Dr Gregory.'

Meg said, 'Would you like me to speak to Morag?'

'Not yet. Let's hope she lets the whole thing die down. The worry is that other people heard the accusation —you know what happens in a small place. Tales are passed round, and folk say there's no smoke without fire.'

'So you want to do nothing?' Mrs Blyth handed them both a mug of coffee. 'Nothing at all, doctor?'

'Perhaps I'd better have a word with the FPC,' Rory decided. 'Just let them know there might be an unreasonable complaint brought in.'

'I'll get them for you.' Mrs Blyth picked up the phone.

Rory turned to Meg. Wearily he said, 'Auntie's prescription, is it? Here you are.' It was already written out, and he signed it and handed it to her.

She said sympathetically, 'Cheer up, Rory. I'll be a character witness.'

He managed a smile. 'I'd like to go for a long walk, but no way, with Greg away. Calls to do, and then stay close to a telephone in case of emergencies. Thank the Lord for good old Jessie. She's out doing repeat calls now.'

Meg stood up. 'Well, I don't suppose I can help. But at least you have Craigie House behind you.'

Rory said suddenly, 'Meg, maybe I could come round tonight? For a drop of Auntie's malt? And maybe—if you're not busy—maybe you'd come out and have a meal somewhere?'

Meg's heart somersaulted. All right, a meal didn't mean a proposal. But it was a wonderful and thrilling and perfect idea—even though she had a feeling she would just be reinforcing Grace's role as auntie. 'Sounds nice.' She hoped she didn't show the joy in her voice. After all these weeks, Rory was asking her—and her alone—to go out with him. It had taken an emergency in the surgery—but so what? If Meg was the right person —the person he wanted to talk to above all others—then that was fine by her. 'See you later, then.'

He seemed pleased. 'Dr Ross from Anstruther will be on call from seven. I'll see you at one minute past!' They were both laughing, and feeling a lot less fraught about Morag Campbell's immature accusation, when the telephone rang.

Mrs Blyth said, 'It'll be the Family Practitioner Committee. They were going to ring back.'

'Right.' Rory picked up the phone. 'Henderson here.' His face changed at once. There was agony in his voice. 'My God! I'll be there. But get an ambulance!' He dashed the phone down. 'It's Jessie! Came off the road at Fountain's End. Will you come, Meg?'

'Right.' She stuffed the prescription in her anorak pocket and followed him in a state of stricken unbelief, to the scarlet sports car. Suddenly she was glad he had a fast vehicle. They drove like the damned through the village, all thoughts of Morag forgotten. Jessie—the most valued friend, the best nurse . . . The call had come from a strange and isolated man who had a smallholding out in the fields between Crail and Anstruther, up on unmade roads.

He was standing by the Land Rover, which had come off the road. Jessie had been thrown out on the road, and lay with pale face, closed eyes, and blood seeping from her nose, her face already blue with bruising. 'I didna turn her over in case it was dangerous. It looks bad, doctor.'

Rory wasted no time asking questions, but knelt by the prostrate form. He made sure her breathing was unrestricted, and there were no broken bones, and took her pulse, which was pitifully weak, before listening very carefully to her chest. 'Shock, Meg. Look out for the ambulance—they'll have plasma.' He tested her reflexes as she lay in the recovery position. Jessie moaned slightly, her eyelids quivered, then sank back again into unconsciousness. 'Poor lass. She can't have put her seat-belt on—so many calls, I suppose she didn't have time.'

The ambulance could be heard from far off, siren wailing. Rory had the needle in a vein as they brought a bag of plasma, connected to a drip. Rory went with Jessie as the stretcher was carried inside. He turned to

Meg from inside the ambulance. 'I must go with her,' he said.

She stood in the chilly road looking up at his strong capable figure. 'Throw me the keys. I'll go back to the surgery and take calls.'

He felt in his pocket, and threw the car keys down to her. 'I'll call you from the hospital.' He turned back at once to his patient.

Meg nodded, her eyes troubled at the stillness of the form on the stretcher. The small ambulance sped down the hill on its journey to Ninewells, the sound of the siren blown occasionally on the wind. Meg looked up at the man. 'Did you see what happened?' she asked.

'No. But I wondered if maybe she tried to avoid the chickens.' His free range hens were wandering about, scratching at the hard ground.

'It's like her.' Meg looked at the overturned Land Rover. 'The road was icy here. Have you called the police?'

The police car was just approaching, and Meg left him explaining just what he had seen. She noticed they were testing the steering wheel as she got into Rory's car and looked at the controls. She found the correct key and started the engine. Her hands were trembling, but she knew she had to get to the surgery. Calls weren't being answered, and that was an offence—one that Rory could do without just now. She roared the engine into life, and steered carefully and doggedly down the brae and back to the little stone surgery in Harbour Lane. Everything was normal there—so quiet and peaceful, with the water lapping at the harbour wall, the boats still there bobbing gently in the cool air.

She parked Rory's car carefully by the empty fishermen's cottages on the front. No one could guess that this morning a hysterical woman had threatened Rory, or that his beloved nurse and right-hand helper was lying critically ill. Meg let herself into the surgery, and sat in the deserted room, looking at the drug company

calendar on the wall, and the list of useful addresses,
like the Hard of Hearing Society, the local Parkinson's
club, and the nearest Drug Dependency Centre. Just
like any other ordinary country GP . . .

Meg realised that the first thing she must do was to let
Grace know where she was. Her head still whirling, she
telephoned, and explained about the accident. She said
nothing about Mrs Campbell—why bother Grace when
there was nothing she could do about it? 'Rory has gone
to the hospital. I'll have to stay here until Mrs Blyth
comes back and can take over the telephone.'

'Don't worry at all about me, lass, Catriona will look
after me. But poor Jessie! We must pray that it's not too
serious. Stay there, Meg. Stay as long as Rory needs
you.'

The sea whispered and swished outside the window.
Meg turned her attention to tidying the papers strewn
over Rory's desk as he rushed away. Then the phone
rang, and she prayed that it was something she would be
able to deal with. 'Yes?'

'Rory dear, I've just had the strangest tale about you
from one of my patients. I know it can't be true, darling,
but I thought you ought to know.'

Her coolness angered Meg. 'Hello, Caroline. Meg
Mackenzie speaking—Rory is out on an emergency.'

'I didn't know you were working there, Meg.' The
voice was distant, as though Caroline was speaking to
someone she didn't know.

'I wasn't. But Jessie came off the road. I'll stay here
until other help can be found.'

'I see. Well, my news can wait.'

'I expect it will be about the Campbells. We thought it
would be all over the village by lunchtime.'

'Er, yes. It—it was about Morag Campbell.'

'I think we ought to leave the ravings of a silly girl until
after we hear how Jessie is, Caroline.' Meg had a certain
satisfaction from putting the phone down on Caroline
Forbes. But she sighed deeply as she did so. The ugly

story was indeed being carried, like an ink stain, around on the feet of anyone who touched on it.

She replaced the receiver, but it rang almost as soon as she put it down. 'Hello?'

'Meg—Rory. They've just completed the neurology examination. The skull is cracked, but there's no brain damage, thank God. She's recovered consciousness, and apart from a headache, she feels OK. I'll be coming home soon. Any urgent calls?'

'No.'

'Meg, Jessie was on the way to Nethergate Grange,' Rory told her. 'I took her medical bag from her car and put it in mine. Do you think you could get another nurse from headquarters to take over? They'll let us have a replacement until she's better.'

'I'll see to it. I brought her bag in with me.'

'Good lass! I'll get back as soon as I can.' He didn't thank her, she noticed. Still, he hadn't had an easy morning, and she could hardly expect him to be thinking of his manners when so much had gone wrong.

She looked up the number of the district nurses, and explained that Jessie was out of action. 'Dr Henderson was wondering if someone else could come and fill in. He's single-handed here,' she told them.

'Oh dear, I'm afraid we can't at the moment. There's no one free until they come off duty at five. We're short-staffed just now, because of 'flu. I'm awfully sorry. Will you let me know if the doctor can manage? Otherwise I'll get someone to come along at five.'

'Five?' That wouldn't do. Not for the diabetics—nor for the epileptics. 'Look, never mind today. As soon as I get relief at the telephone, I'll go along to Nethergate myself,' Meg decided.

'You're a nurse? That's a blessing, then. I can't see us being much help to you this week at least.'

'All right, don't worry about it.' Meg rang off, and went at once to Jessie's list of calls in her leather bag. She phoned the Grange. 'Do you have the ampoules there?

Jessie can't come, and I'll do the injections if you have the stuff.'

'Oh, Sister Mackenzie, that's real kind. Yes, we have all the drugs in a locked cupboard—Jessie had the key.'

Meg went through the bag and found a bunch of three keys. She was just studying the list, and seeing who else had to be seen apart from Nethergate Grange, when Mrs Blyth came puffing through the door. 'Any calls?' she asked.

Meg pulled on her extra jersey and explained what she was doing. She took Jessie's bag, her fingers cold round the leather handle, and ran up the lane to Craigie House. Telling her story yet again, she found the keys to her own little Metro, and pulled out the choke, praying that it would start. At the third turn, it grumbled into life. She looked again at the list and realised that she still had Rory's car keys in the pocket of her slacks. She drove down to the harbour once more and left the keys with Mrs Blyth. And at that moment a taxi drew up, and Rory stepped out, looking tired and dishevelled.

'What are you doing?' he wanted to know.

She looked at him, her temper short. 'I'm going to see Nethergate Grange, Mrs Moore, Mrs Elgin and Mr Millar, as far as I know. There's no one else free.' She jumped into the Metro and started it up again.

Rory stood looking after her, and she felt regret at snapping at him, but had no time to worry about it. It was a long drive to the Grange, and Mrs Elgin's farm was isolated among the distant countryside past Abercrombie. It was a glorious drive in summer—and in autumn too, when the leaves were changing. But when you were in a hurry, and sick people needed injections, it became only a chore. It was a worry too, as she had not seen these patients, and would have to check Jessie's book carefully to make sure of the treatment.

It was six in the afternoon by the time she had seen all Jessie's patients. She coasted back to Craigie House, only to remember that Grace's prescription was still in her pocket, and she needed her tablets that night. She drove to the pharmacist, he would have the bottles ready; he was efficient with his regulars. Meg dragged her feet as she stumbled over the threshold into the cosy little shop, that smelt of cough medicine and baby powder and scented soap.

She was just going to the counter when she realised that the shop was unnaturally full for this time of the evening. And it was soon painfully clear why the customers were hanging about gossiping. As she waited miserably for the pills, Miss Laughton and Miss Williamson were anxious to pass on the news. 'Did you ken that the doctor made a pass at Morag Campbell? Young Rory Henderson, no less. There's going to be a case, you ken.'

Meg snapped, 'It's a lie!'

Miss Laughton turned to Mrs Pittaway, who was nodding her birdlike head in excitement. 'Och, she would say that, now, would she no, her being sweet on the doctor herself?'

Meg said more calmly, 'It's a lie, Miss Laughton, and there are witnesses to prove it. So be careful of your tongue the now, or the rooks will be having it.' And she took her bottles from the chemist and swept out of the shop, her cheeks hot with anger. She knew that by next morning the story would have circulated through the entire population, and her excuses would have been either totally ignored or discounted because she herself was sweet on the doctor. So much for village life!

Grace was there, with her gentle voice and wise old head. 'Catriona has made your favourite broth. Now get into a hot bath and come down in your dressing gown for your supper, my dear. We must look after our working girl.'

'It isn't the work, Auntie, it's the people. They do——'

'Get away upstairs this minute! We've got plenty of time to be talking when you come down.'

'Thanks, Auntie.' Meg did as she was told, content to have someone who cared enough to scold her like a child. She soaked in steaming bath oil, and came down in her fluffy dressing gown, her hair damp on her shoulders, but her feelings calmer, and her thoughts straightened out a little. Over hot soup and cottage pie, she told the full story. 'I doubt there'll be anyone in the surgery tomorrow—none of the casual ones, anyway. Mrs Campbell will have frightened them all off. Poor Rory!'

'It will pass, my dear,' soothed Grace. 'Are you to help out tomorrow too?'

'I'll have to. There's no one else.' Meg looked across at Grace. 'I say, you don't need me, do you?'

'I can manage very well with Caddy. I like to see you doing what you're trained for, Meg. I've been telling you for months that you ought to be nursing.'

'Well, at least tomorrow I'll get the calls over in the morning, so that I can be here for you in the afternoon.' Meg ate for a while, relishing the good meal. 'Rory hasn't actually asked me for help, you know.'

'He knows you're part of the family, so he assumes you'll be on his side, just as Flora and I are.'

'That's right. He did say he'd come round—when I told him Craigie House was behind him.' Then Meg realised something else. 'He even asked me to go out for dinner! I forgot!' She put down her fork, but as she looked at the clock, she knew that Rory had forgotten too. She smiled a bit sadly. 'Och, well, maybe he'll ask me again.'

'I'm certain he will,' Grace agreed.

They all went to bed early, exhausted by the stress of the unexpected accident, plus the unprovoked attack by Mrs Campbell. Meg thought she wouldn't sleep for worrying, but tiredness overtook her, and she slept almost at once.

She was at the surgery in Harbour Lane at the same time as Mrs Blyth next morning. The older woman opened the door with her key, and hurried to put on the gas fire, for the wind was rough and cold, creeping under the doors, and even through the double glazing. The place soon warmed up, though the noise made by the wind was unnervingly loud. Mrs Blyth put the kettle on and opened up the waiting room, but nobody came.

They said nothing as they drank their first cup of tea, and Meg went through the list of necessary calls. 'You might as well set off. Doctor will probably be late in, as he was up in the night with Mrs Dougall's ulcer.' Mrs Blyth had found a night visit form Rory must have left some time while the rest of the village slept.

Meg had brought her thick anorak with her, and now she buttoned it to the neck. 'I'll telephone from Nethergate to make sure there are no more calls,' she said.

'This is really very good of you, Meg. Doctor'll be grateful.'

'What are friends for?' She forced open the door against the might of the wind, and drove carefully up to the main road, turning past Craigie House on her long journey to the Grange. The waves were very wild, throwing up huge walls of spray and drenching the road before slipping down again and collecting themselves for another assault. Meg kept her hands firmly on the steering wheel, and tried not to use the brakes too much—memories of the pathetic little Land Rover, its four wheels up in the air, its owner whipped off under that red blanket by white-faced ambulancemen.

When she phoned from the Grange, it was almost midday, though with the lowering clouds, one could hardly have guessed. Mrs Blyth answered the phone. 'Doctor's with Dr Whyte—the man from the FPC,' she told Meg. 'Mrs Campbell did complain, and apparently there's got to be a hearing of some kind. It's in the rules.'

'That's daft,' protested Meg. 'With you as a witness? Waste of time.'

'No, apparently because I answered the telephone during the examination, there's a reasonable doubt.'

A sudden crazy idea came to Meg, and she spoke on

impulse. 'I was there too, Mrs Blyth. Don't you remember? I was in the office chatting to you when you had to go through for the examination, and I saw the whole thing. If Morag had objected, we'd both have heard something.'

The woman hesitated. 'I know you brought the prescription requests in that day, but didn't you leave when I went into the consulting room?'

'No.' Meg had never lied in her life, but she almost saw herself in that office—a corroborating voice that would save Rory from further harassment. Her hand trembled, but she went on, 'You can tell Dr Whyte I was there too. With two witnesses, surely there's no need of a hearing.'

'I'll tell him.' Mrs Blyth sounded relieved. 'There are no more calls, so no need to come back here. Thanks for your help, lassie.'

Meg grimaced as she put the phone down. 'Everything OK at base camp?' Matron of Nethergate was a cheerful soul. Meg assured her that all was well, and drove back through the wind and the driving rain to Craigie House.

She didn't tell Grace what she had done, even though the old lady would fully understand, but later that day she heard Rory's car draw up with a screech of brakes outside, and his running footsteps coming up the path. She heard him ask Caddy where she was.

'I'm upstairs, Rory!' she called.

He came to the foot of the stairs and looked up, his handsome face shadowed, his eyes angry and his hair dishevelled. 'Come away down, Meg, if you don't mind.' She met his look from the landing, and there was no refusing that masterful figure. She shook her hair back and walked as calmly as she could down the graceful staircase, the deep red carpet masking any sound of her feet. She stood at the bottom, looking up at him, as he took her shoulders in both strong hands. 'There is no way you are going to perjure yourself for me, Meg Mackenzie!' he grated.

CHAPTER FIVE

MEG MACKENZIE looked up at the towering figure of Dr Henderson as he stood very close to her in the shadowy hall of Craigie House. It was after six, and getting dark, the wind still whispering and whistling in the trees outside, and along the draughty passages. 'It has nothing at all to do with you, Rory Henderson!' she snapped.

'I see. I'm the one who's being slandered, and you say it has nothing to do with me? That's rich!' His tone too was irritable.

'I'm not perjuring myself. And if I were, it would no be for you. It would be for justice. I can't stand unfairness—especially to a good man.'

'I don't want you to interfere! Mrs Blyth has already told Dr Whyte that you were there in the surgery. I want you to telephone and tell him you were mistaken about the time.'

'Don't speak to me like a schoolkid, Dr High and Mighty!' Meg snapped. 'What I do is my affair, and I want you to get that very clear.'

'But it's daft, Meg—or can't you see that? Crazy!'

'You're not the rugby captain now, you can't boss the wee kids like you used to. I know what I saw that day in the surgery, and I'm going to say so. If there's nothing else you wish to say, then good night to you!'

He shrugged his shoulders then, broad and protective, somehow, in the big dark house. Meg saw that she had won. Rory said, 'I can't leave without saying hello to Auntie. Is she in the drawing room?'

'Yes, she is. And don't be going and telling her that we've been arguing, it'll upset her.'

He paused at the door, looked back, and hissed, 'I haven't been arguing. It was you who was pigheaded!'

And he opened the door before Meg had time to reply. Seething, she followed him into the room, which was warm with both radiators and a wood fire burning. Rory went to his aunt and kissed her. 'Just passing. How are you, dear? You are nice and cosy in here.'

'I'm fine. Will you take a dram, Rory?'

'A wee one, thanks.' He helped himself. As he sat down, Meg went over to the trolley and helped herself, thus forcing Rory to apologise for not asking her if she wanted a drink. 'You usually say no.'

'That's a bit of a lame excuse.' But she said it sweetly, so as not to alert Grace to their argument.

But Grace was not to be fooled. She said quietly, 'Miss MacFarlane was here this afternoon, Rory. I've heard all about the Campbells. Nobody believes it, of course —your character is well known. No one can think it will go to a hearing. I really can't think what made them do it.'

Meg gave Rory a long challenging look, and he shrugged again. 'I believe it has to, Auntie. Because Mrs Blyth took a phone call, so she had to look away.'

Grace shook her head. 'The girls today are as high-spirited as the laddies. Someone should have a wee word with Morag. She'll probably speak up before she has to go to a hearing, when it will be her word against yours, Rory.' She turned to look at Meg, who was sipping her whisky and Highland water. 'Surely it's nothing for you two to quarrel about.'

There was a silence, during which they each waited for the other to own up. Meg stole a glance at Rory, who was staring into the fire as though reading some magic legend there. Meg broke the silence. 'I think he just called in to thank me for helping out at the surgery, Auntie.'

'That's right,' agreed the young doctor quickly. 'And to bring you the news about Jessie.'

'How is she, poor dear? And what can I send for her? Is she allowed to eat fruit?' Grace was concerned. 'Miss MacFarlane has posted a get-well card from us both, but we would like to send something to the hospital.'

'They want to keep her in for at least three weeks,' Rory told her.

'Oh, my goodness! Is her skull really fractured, then?'

'There's a hairline fracture. It's just for her own good, really.' Rory added, 'I'm sorry to be asking you, Meg, but I'd be—grateful—if you could come and help us out till the end of the week.'

'I'll do that, Rory.' She pretended to sound condescending, although she already knew that she was enjoying the work, and would happily stay for the full three weeks.

Just then the telephone rang, and Meg jumped up. 'I'll take it in the hall, while you go on with your chat,' she said sweetly. She could tell by the set of Rory's shoulders that he was still agitated about her decision to testify. But she felt it was impossible to go back on her word now. She picked up the receiver. It was Alistair Reid.

'Meg, about Morag Campbell.'

'Yes, Alistair?'

'Would it do any good, do you think, if I went to the house and pleaded with her better nature?'

'It might. I'd thought about that. Or else meet her accidentally at the Scarlet Flamingo? The informal approach might work—away from her mother's influence?'

'Then shall we go along together?' he suggested. 'She's usually there every night, is she not?'

'Right. Why not? We'll go along at about eight.'

Meg went back to the drawing room filled with hope. She and Alistair often chatted with the kids at the café. This was an idea that might work. 'I'll be going out at eight,' she told them.

Rory stood up. 'Then I won't hold up your dinner. Good night to you both.' As she saw him out, he asked, 'Where are you going?'

'Don't ask me as though I was going to do something foolish, Rory!'

He turned away, exasperated. 'All right, don't tell me.'

'I won't.' But as he went down the steps, Meg's tender heart was touched. 'Don't fret. Things will turn out.'

And he turned from the gate to say with resignation, 'Leave it to wee Meg, is that what you're telling me?'

She smiled. 'More or less. 'Night.'

Grace demanded the moment she returned, 'What on earth are you cooking, Meg?'

'I've been a little bit naughty,' Meg confessed.

'Then I'd better have a sherry to calm my nerves.'

Meg poured her a small sherry, and explained, 'I let Dr Whyte know I was there during the examination. I wasn't there in body—but in spirit—well, you know. I was morally there. Because I'm certain that Rory is innocent.'

Meg waited, hardly breathing, for Grace to explode. But the old lady sipped her drink before saying slowly, 'That's taking loyalty a bit far, lassie. Specially for someone you're always arguing with!' There was a gleam in her eyes that made Meg breathe out with relief. 'I'd probably have done the same thing—but I do hope you won't be called under oath.'

'I hope it won't get that far. Alistair and I are going to have a word with Morag tonight—that might work.' And the subject was closed for the moment.

The minister had no doubt at all of Rory's innocence. 'I haven't known him as long as the rest of you, but he's a most upright and excellent doctor. The child must be hysterical or something!'

'Her mother was, this morning,' Meg told him. 'My guess is that the girl had to find some explanation for the marks—and with such a straitlaced mother, she thought she would accuse someone of doing it against her will. But you've seen her with her boyfriend, Alistair—that lad must have done it. They're always clinging on to one another, and kissing and cuddling.'

'Ah yes—the young man with the blue streak in his

hair, and a skull and crossbones on his jacket.'

'That's the one. Think you can get through to him?'

Alistair grinned. 'I have to, Meg. It's my duty.'

Meg squeezed his arm as they walked along in the blustery darkness. 'I'll be with you. I'll help.'

'All for one, eh? Like the Three Musketeers? I hope it doesn't come to weapons.'

'Let's not talk about that.' They strode out together, the lights of the Scarlet Flamingo visible for a long way along the flat road. Meg did indeed begin to feel a little nervous. The young people had always appeared peaceable enough, but she was aware that aggression existed. She must rely on her long acquaintance with the local youngsters, and their previous good neighbourliness together.

They pushed open the door, and the warmth and the loud music hit them at the same time. The café wasn't full, but there were six or seven couples, and a group of four bike boys in a corner, laughing a lot, drinking lager. The two conspirators took a seat at an inconspicuous table, and Alistair bought two coffees. 'Well, partner, what do we do now? She isn't here.'

Meg said, 'She'll probably come. The young ones haven't been gossiping about the affair like the villagers have. Morag probably thinks she's been very clever at the moment, so she won't feel the need to hide in a corner. In fact, if I know her, she'll be proud of what she's done to Rory.'

Alistair shook his head. 'What a pity the days of a good hiding are over.'

But at that moment Morag and her boyfriend came into the café. They didn't look around, but went straight to the bar, and asked for white wine. Meg and Alistair looked at each other for support. 'Who goes first?' asked Meg.

Alistair said nervously, 'You can't rush this sort of thing.'

'If I don't rush it, I'll run away.' Meg stood up, took a

deep breath, and went over to the couple. 'Hi.'

Morag turned round. She showed no emotion, and Meg realised she didn't know that Meg was working at the surgery. Meg explained, 'I was at Dr Henderson's this morning. I'm his district nurse while Mrs Peebles is in hospital. I was there when your mother called.'

The girl's face changed under its heavy make-up, and she swore. '—— off.'

The boy demanded in a broad Dundee accent, 'What's all this, then? Who's she?'

Morag grabbed him. 'Never you mind. Come over here.' And she pulled him with her to the other side of the room.

Alistair was at Meg's side in a moment. 'She won't communicate, will she?'

'Exactly.' Meg was determined then. She wasn't very tall, and she wasn't very strong, but that child wasn't getting away without knowing what she had done. She strode across the floor, and not giving Morag the chance to speak or the room to get away, said in a clear voice, 'You've told a bad lie to save yourself. Morag, if you speak the truth now, it won't hurt you. If you go on with this play-acting, you won't win, and it will hurt both you and your family. I hope you get my meaning.' She stood back then, as they both stared at her, speechless. 'I came to help, you know. It's for the best.'

She walked to the door, then, and went out. She turned to see where Alistair was, and saw both teenagers listening to something he was saying. In a moment he had joined Meg outside, and they started back, leaning now against the wind as they walked. After a while, Alistair said, 'I don't think it will work. It's just made her the centre of attention, and I think the child is enjoying it.'

At the gate of Craigie House they paused. Meg said, 'Thank you for backing me up.'

Alistair seemed to have forgotten why they had been

out. 'I've been thinking, Meg—it would be nice if you'd come out with me for the day. I—how about lunch in Edinburgh on Saturday?'

Her heart sank. Please don't invite me out, she thought silently. Aloud she had an excuse. 'I'm playing squash for the team,' she explained.

'Is that a regular thing?' he asked.

'Er—not every Saturday. But I might have a steady place soon.'

He seemed to guess she was trying not to encourage him. He said with a gentle smile, 'Then maybe I'll join the squash club.'

'Why not?' Meg tried to keep her voice light, but the wind whipped the words out of her mouth. 'I'd better go in, Alistair. I have to be at the surgery early in the morning.'

When she went in, Catriona had bathed Grace and helped her to bed. Meg tapped on the door, where the light was still on. 'I'm sorry to be late.'

'Don't be—Caddy has helped me very well. Any luck at Jimmy's?' Grace had stayed awake to hear her progress. Meg had to admit that they had not got through to Morag Campbell's conscience. Grace said, 'Pity. I'm so very fond of Rory—and I believe he might have decided to stay on here if this hadn't happened.' She patted Meg's hand with her good one. 'You did the right thing, Meg. But I'm afraid Dr Whyte is the next step—an FPC hearing. You've involved yourself in that now.' Grace's pale face twisted suddenly, and sweat appeared on her forehead.

'Chest pain, Auntie? Shall I get you a tablet?' Meg hastily shook out a white GNT and placed it under Grace's tongue. It usually settled her angina pains within a few seconds. She sat with her, smoothing her forehead. The tablet was taking longer than usual to work. 'I'll call Rory!'

'No.' Grace whispered it through white lips.

'I must. The pain should have gone by now.'

'I'm an old woman, it's only to be expected.' But Grace gasped after the strain of saying so much. Her face was as white as her pillow. Meg ran to the telephone.

A woman's voice answered—Caroline Forbes. Meg gritted her teeth. So he had feminine solace, did he? 'I need Rory urgently!' she said.

'Is that Meg Mackenzie?'

'Yes. Hurry! It's Auntie Grace.'

'Rory here. What is it, Meg?'

'It's her heart,' Meg told him. 'The pain hasn't cleared with GNT. She's had it for—' she looked down at her watch in the shadowy hall, but the grandfather clock chimed the time for her, 'she's had it for nearly half an hour now.'

'I'm on the way. Call the ambulance, Meg.'

Meg did as she was told, then ran upstairs again, leaving the front door open to the wild wind. Grace tried to protest, but she was too weak, Meg collected her few necessities for hospital. She had foreseen that it might be needed, and had kept the things neatly in a drawer for just such a sad moment. Her eyes were full of tears as she folded the best fluffy dressing gown and laid it on top of the bag.

Rory bounded up the stairs. 'It's all right, Auntie, I'm here.' To Meg he nodded after testing Grace's pulse and taking her blood pressure. 'I'll go with her, Meg. It's an infarct.'

'May I come?'

'Will you drive after the ambulance, to bring us home?'

'I will.'

Grace was carried, a tiny figure under the blankets, out to the ambulance. Meg locked the door of Craigie House, murmuring, 'Please God she will come back.' It was no surprise that her weak heart had failed, yet such was her youth of personality that it was hard to see her helpless. Meg took Rory's car, because it was already out in the road. She followed the tail lights of the ambulance. Rory was taking no chances; he was admitting Grace to Dundee, where the most modern treatment was, and where the consultant already knew Grace's history. Meg drove that night faster than she ever had in her life, following those vivid tail lights, and that flashing blue one, that she saw in her mind's eye for nights afterwards. The blue light, and the howling wind . . .

Rory and Meg sat together silent, waiting for news from the consultant. The night was wild, the corridors shadowy, eerie in the small hours of the night. Figures moved behind screens, and voices murmured. Rory turned to whisper to Meg, 'She is eighty, you know.' He handed her a handkerchief.

'I'm not crying for her—for myself . . .'

'I know, Meg, I know. She's more to you than your father, I know.'

'She's more to the whole town. Everyone was her family . . .'

'Hush, love, you'll upset yourself more. She might recover, you know.'

'I suppose there's no way you can know yet?' sniffed Meg.

'Not yet.' Rory put his arm round her. Much later a nurse brought them a cup of tea, and offered them a rest room, but they refused to move from the ward.

Dawn was breaking, and with it a respite from the wind, when a red-eyed houseman came out to them. 'She's stable. She's sleeping now, and we think she'll pull through. But she's a frail little thing. Would you like to come back this evening?'

'We've come from Brathay, over twenty miles. But we'll come back between surgeries.' Rory stood up and shook hands with the houseman and thanked him. 'I can get Dr Ross to help me on call. Come away, Meg. We can do no more.'

'May I just see her?' asked Meg.

The houseman broke the rules. 'Of course.'

Meg put her head round the door. Grace was connected to a monitor. She looked peaceful now, after the lines of agony that had been etched in her face when the attack first started. Meg put her hand over Grace's thin one. It was warm—that was a good sign. She turned and blindly followed Rory down to the car.

Rory drove back. They didn't speak. The sunrise was beautiful, rising from the sea in a hazy blur of pink and orange and yellow in the pale blue November day, merging with the ocean so that there was no knowing where the horizon was. Catriona was up, her plump face blotchy with weeping. She made them tea and toast, then Rory fell asleep where he was in the armchair in the kitchen, and Meg with her head on her arms on the kitchen table. The grandfather clock struck five, six and seven without anyone hearing it.

At half past eight Meg stirred. She looked up, remembering with a rush that the big old house was without its mistress, and although the morning was bright with the gaiety of frost in a clear sky, it felt bleak and alone. She looked across the kitchen, where Rory still slept, a look of helplessness about him, his black locks tousled around his head, his shirt crumpled under the sweater.

As quietly as she could, she shook the ash from the fire and relit it with the rolled paper and logs that Caddy always left ready. She spooned coffee into the filter and switched on the machine, which was soon bubbling and spluttering. Rory opened his eyes. For a moment neither spoke, then he stood up suddenly and caught her against him. Meg wound her arms round his strong body, her fingers curling in the soft wool of his sweater. After a long time he whispered, 'I'll phone the hospital. Pour the coffee, Meg. We've got to get moving.'

There was no change in Grace; that at least meant she was holding her own. Meg said, 'I'm glad we're going to be busy. I couldn't just sit and wait.'

He smiled, a new look of respect and affection in the

blue eyes. 'We're going to be busy all right. I'd better get up to Greg's place and find myself a clean shirt. See you in the surgery.'

But the new Rory quickly vanished during morning surgery. The moment Meg arrived she heard voices outside, and a man staggered in with blood trickling from a cut on his head. She ran to him, took him through to the couch, though Rory had not yet arrived. The man said, 'No, I'm all right. My wife—in the car—skidded on the ice—she's unconscious—God, I don't know if she's breathing!'

Meg left Mrs Blyth to comfort the man with tea and sympathy, while Meg grabbed Jessie Peebles' little leather bag and ran up the brae to where the man said his car had come off the road. It was off the road indeed, completely upside down. The woman had been lifted out, but left on the grass while the man ran for help. Meg checked her carefully. She was breathing, and her pulse was all right. No limbs seemed broken. Meg looked around. What did she do now? Then she remembered Grace's wheelchair. They were not far from Craigie House, and she ran quickly along the road, explained to Catriona what was happening, and got the woman, moaning and vomiting, into the chair, wheeling her gently down to the surgery, where she took her husband's place on the couch. She was left to recover while Meg dressed the man's cut head.

Patients began to arrive. Meg was still wearing what she had had on last night, though she had managed to wash her face and brush her hair. Still no sign of Rory. She decided that the accident victim ought to have a skull X-ray, and rang to arrange for the ambulance to take her along.

The man objected. 'I want to see about my car—it isna locked.'

Meg calmed him. 'I'll get the garage to take it there,' she assured him.

'Is it an expensive garage?'

Meg gave him a hard stare. 'It's the only garage. Please go with your wife—I've done what I can for you. We have patients waiting, the doctor has been up all night, and I have to go to Nethergate Grange in twenty minutes.'

Rory swept in. 'God, Meg, couldn't you have attended to some of these patients? The waiting room's full!'

'I've just been attending to two RTA patients!' She tried not to snap, but it was no use. At that moment the ambulance arrived, and the man came out of Rory's room, protesting that his car had to be seen to.

Rory took charge, muttering to Mrs Blyth as Meg telephoned the garage.

'I wouldn't mind, but half these people waiting have nothing wrong with them. They've come to see the monster that Morag Campbell thinks I am.'

'Are you ready for the first?' asked Mrs Blyth.

'Send her in. Meg, have you got the list of calls?'

'Yes. I'll get on with them.' They spoke as distant colleagues, suddenly. The closeness of last night was lost in the hurly-burly of a busy surgery.

The woman who had gone in said, 'My problem is really a woman's. Can I talk to the nurse?'

'Come back, Meg!' But she had heard the request, and was already back in the consulting room.

The woman worked in the grocer's. 'I'm not ill, but my sister's two laddies have just been diagnosed as having muscular dystrophy. They're in Australia, and I've just had the letter.'

Meg said, 'This is the doctor's business. He'll refer you to the geneticist, and they'll counsel you about having a family yourself. That's what you want to know, isn't it? If any children you might have will be affected?'

'Aye, Sister. But the only thing is—I think I'm pregnant now.'

'Oh, my dear . . .' Meg brushed her hair back from her face. 'I'd better give you a note to go for a pregnancy test. But you must go through to get an appointment made for you by Dr Henderson to see the geneticist.'

Rory was sympathetic. He arranged an appointment by telephone for the woman. The waiting room was fuller than she had ever seen it, and Meg was glad to get out into the sharp morning air. She drove with extreme caution, as she passed the upturned vehicle in the field just past Craigie House. The road bent a lot, and was still covered with black ice. It took twice as long to get to Nethergate Grange.

When she had done her injections and dressings, she phoned the surgery. Rory answered, sounding distinctly annoyed. 'This fellow has decided to sue the council for not putting signs up to say the road bends sharply at that place where the accident happened.'

'But the road bends all the way,' protested Meg.

'Why must we get the tiresome ones just when we're busy enough for three?' he demanded.

Meg knew he was only blowing off steam, and that he didn't intend to shout. 'So there's nothing else for me to do. Shall I come back to the surgery?'

'Yes. There's a man waiting to have his ears syringed, and a young lad has a nasty cut on his knee that will need stitching. He's in the treatment room. And for goodness' sake, don't drive fast, or you'll end up like Jessie. But get here as fast as you can.'

By the time Meg got back to the surgery, and had syringed the waiting ears, Rory was on the phone again. He called her in. 'That pregnancy test is positive. She'll need to have her creatine kinase assessed. Get her on the phone, please. She's gone back to work, she'll be in the shop.' He turned to the pile of letters and papers on the desk. 'She ought to have had the test as soon as she got married.'

'She's only just heard,' Meg explained. 'Her sister lives in Australia.'

Rory sighed, and began to tidy the letters. Mrs Blyth brought in more coffee, and between them they tidied the place up, and Meg filed the cards while Mrs Blyth took dictation for letters for patients who had been seen that morning.

When Meg looked at her watch, it was two o'clock. 'If there's nothing else, I'll away home,' she said. Home. Craigie House wasn't home without Grace.

Rory scarcely glanced up from his work. She left the surgery quietly, driving the few yeards up Harbour Lane, and along to Craigie House. Catriona was sitting in the kitchen, with sadness in her eyes. 'I didna think you'd be wanting a meal,' she apologised.'

'Not to worry—I'll take a sandwich.' Meg helped herself to fresh rolls and shrimp paste. 'There's been no call from the hospital?'

'Nothing.'

They sat for a while in silence; Meg's eyes began to close. But then she remembered she had not told Alistair that Grace was in hospital. 'I'll just ring to get an up-to-date report on Auntie, then I'll let the minister know,' she said.

'He'll want to put her on the list to be remembered in our prayers.' Catriona was very subdued. 'I never really expected her to be ill. It's awful, being without her.'

'Caddy, why not take a few days off? Meg suggested suddenly. 'Go and see your folks. You're not going to be doing much if you stay here.'

'Maybe I will—thanks.'

Meg dialled Alistair's number. With Caddy gone too, Craigie House would be very lonely.

'I'll come round.' The young minister was eager to do his duty and call on the afflicted, and for once, Meg didn't mind. She knew he would speak sensibly. Rory was too busy to have time for her, and Catriona had little conversation at all. She had only liked being here because Grace was such good company.

Alistair arrived as Catriona was leaving. They went into the kitchen, and Meg put a log on the fire and the kettle on the stove. 'Thank you for coming,' she said.

'It's my job, Meg—but more than that, we're friends, aren't we?'

'Yes.' She managed a smile. 'Yes, we are.'

'So relax. In fact, try to rest a little. If you like, I'll come with you to the hospital.'

'Oh, but Rory . . .' Meg stopped.

'You don't have to go with Rory. He's a busy man. I have lots of time to spare, Meg. And you know how much I want to help you.'

His voice was very sincere. And Meg was tired, upset, and had been snapped at all morning by an irritable Rory. She poured two mugs of tea, and brought one to Alistair in the armchair. Then she took hers and sat on the rug at his feet, watching the flames licking around the fragrant wood. 'It's been a dreadful few hours,' she sighed. 'I can hardly believe that so much has happened. It isn't even twenty-four hours since Grace was taken ill, yet it seems almost a lifetime away.'

'And you've done nothing but work, Meg.' Alistair was so very sympathetic and gentle. A caring person, a man to rely on. 'You must find some time to rest.' He reached out and drew her into the circle of his arms. She leaned her head on his knee, as his soft voice went on, explaining, understanding . . . 'You've been more than a daughter to her, Meg. Without your constant care, Grace Henderson would not have lived so long. She told me when I first came to Craigie House that she didn't have long to go.'

Meg looked up. 'She told you that?'

'Yes. You didn't know?'

'She didn't tell me, but perhaps I didn't want to see it. I needed her so much—her wisdom, and her warmth, and her sense of humour . . . Oh, Alistair, how on earth can I go on without——' and as she bent her head again, the young man pulled her closer and kissed the top of her head, her forehead, her cheek . . .

'Don't tell me not to love you, Meg, because I can't help it,' he muttered.

'I'm too tired to argue with you now. And I'm so grateful for your company and the way you always seem to understand how I feel.'

'Then don't. Sleep, my dear. You can argue with me another day.' But as she obeyed him, and allowed her consciousness to drift away, Meg felt a great yearning for the man she had argued with all morning. It was wrong to let Alistair stay while her heart was crying out for someone else. But she had no physical reserves left, and she fell fast asleep in the arms of Alistair Reid. The grandfather clock ticked away in the hall—and Grace Henderson lay on the brink of life and death, unable to decide which way to choose.

CHAPTER SIX

Jessie didn't come back to work immediately, though she was home from hospital. Rory seemed to take it for granted that Meg would stay on. 'Now that you know the patients, it would be kinder for them not to have to get used to yet another nurse,' he explained.

Meg waited for the polite request, but none came, as Rory dived back into his paperwork. She shrugged. 'I'm better off busy. Craigie House is very empty just now.'

Rory spared her a glance. 'It can't be much of a home, Meg. But Grace is holding her own. Perhaps she'll be back with us before long.'

'Is that what they told you?'

'Well—no,' he admitted.

'Then don't patronise me, Rory. I can see well enough how ill she is. I don't want her home until she's well enough, and so far there's no sign of that.'

They had started taking turns to visit. Going together each night was too much. Alternate evenings was better —though the drive was lonelier. Grace was always pleased to see her—but Meg could see what a strain it was to remain chatty for the whole visit. Grace wanted to know if Rory's hearing was due.

'He hasn't heard,' she told her.

'You have seen Morag?'

'I've appealed to her better nature.'

'Then follow her up,' Grace advised. 'Her conscience has been stirred. Try another attack.'

Meg looked down at the frail form. 'Dear Auntie, always thinking of how you can help!'

'You'll have to do it for me, dear. Try again, won't you?'

'I promise.'

But the thought of facing that aggressive child was daunting. Meg was not naturally extrovert. But neither was Alistair—and he had waded in to support her. She must try again—for the sake of Alistair and Grace, as well as poor Rory, who couldn't defend himself, except by his spotless reputation.

That evening, Meg made herself cheese on toast, and thought with nostalgia of Catriona's home-made soup. Life was changing in Brathay. And her own cosy ideas were being jostled—first by Rory Henderson's cutting remarks, and now by reality, as the evidence was produced that life never stayed the same.

She sat alone by the log fire in the kitchen. She never went into the drawing room now—it looked too empty without Grace. She knew she had been given a charge—to go and see Morag Campbell again. Rory would be visiting Grace tonight, so this was her chance to try and help them both. She stood up, and took her sheepskin jacket from behind the door. It was a long walk when the weather was cold, and she dared not invite Alistair—he would take it as encouragement, and she was not so cruel as to urge him on when she was not in love with him. Meg pulled the door tight behind her and set off on the lonely trudge to the garish lights of the Scarlet Flamingo.

She didn't look round when she went in. She bought a coffee and took it to a corner, her heart heavy with sadness over Grace. She knew that sooner or later she would have to make a move—look around for Morag, make the attack on behalf of common-sense and humanity . . . That was why she had come. But depression made her slow; she hugged the cup with both hands, and stared into space.

'You look fair sad. It's Miss Henderson, is it no?'

Meg looked up, surprised that someone should read her mind so well. 'Morag! I thought I wasn't on your visiting list.'

The girl was dressed in black leather, and her eyes

were surrounded by huge rings of black. But she sat down opposite Meg. 'Geoff's working nights, in a garage.' She said without prompting, 'I'm sorry about Miss Henderson. She was a nice lady—not like some of the snotty kirk folks.'

Meg understood; Morag's mother was a tireless worker for the kirk. 'Your mother? Not easy at home? Being leader of the Guild, I guess you feel you have to live up to her image of you?'

Morag looked down, her fingers twisting together on the table. 'She's always talking about standards—but you ken she isna all that Christian at hame. No sympathy with those as ken no better.'

Meg said, suddenly understanding the lassie, 'We're none of us Christians at home. We never live up to what we want people to think.'

'I ken that.' Morag spoke truculently. 'But my mother wants me to have standards she doesna practise herself.' She faced Meg's eyes. 'I think she's ower hard on me.'

Meg said, seeing a hidden plea for help, 'I'm sure. But in a way, it's only because she loves you. It's only natural, if you think about it, to try and protect your daughter.'

They both knew she was talking about her lie about Rory now. Morag whispered, 'Aye.' Meg knew she understood, and waited. She had made her case last time they talked, and Morag wasn't stupid. Meg held her breath; she felt she might at last have got through.

But Morag suddenly stood up, scraping back her chair, and ran over to a group of friends. Meg put her head down. She had failed. There could be no more closeness with Morag Campbell. Grace would ask her, tomorrow night, and she would have to admit she had failed.

She walked back in the drab night, let herself into the back door with the key. There was a small sound by her feet, and she turned when she had put the light on. In the yellow rays was a small black kitten. It mewed again, and

Meg bent to pick it up, when it immediately started purring like a tiny engine. There was a tiny star of white under its chin, and she could feel its little heart beating fast. 'There now, wee one—did you know I was miserable, coming into an empty house? So you came to cheer me up, did you? They do say a black cat is lucky. So come away in, my wee friend, and I'll find you some cream.'

At once she felt better. Even such a small scrap of living creature was something to care for, in this mausoleum of a house. The kitten demolished the cream and headed back to her, purring. She opened a tin of sardines and crumbled one in the saucer. The kitten wolfed it, starving. Meg found a cardboard box and folded a soft scarf in it by the dying embers of the fire. It curled up at once and closed its big blue eyes, the purring lessening as sleep came. Meg touched the small head, a smile on her lips, before putting out the light and going upstairs, her loneliness forgotten.

The telephone shrilled just as she got to the landing, and she ran down again to answer it. 'Rory here.'

Her heart constricted. 'How is she, Rory?'

'Failing.' There was a pause. He said, 'I felt you ought to know.'

'Yes.' Another pause, while she sensed the agony they both shared. 'Does she know?'

'Of course. Can you imagine Grace not knowing?'

'No. Shall I go now? I have to see her.'

'No, let her rest. I'll call for you early in the morning—seven.' He went on hesitantly, 'She's had a happy life. You wouldn't want her to go on in pain.'

Meg smiled in the shadows. 'I'm not a child, Rory.'

'Only trying to help,' he explained.

'I know. But what I'm trying to say is—don't worry about me. God knows you've got enough on your mind at the moment.'

His voice was tender. 'Get some sleep, lass.'

Meg lay in bed, feeling the force of Rory's gentle

words like something she could touch. For all his sharpness in the surgery, he could be tender. Even in her misery about Grace, this was something she could cherish. She had only had a few short weeks since the drama when she almost lost her father. And now her aunt too. Yet this was a much sharper loss, and she felt a great emptiness, a great need for someone, something to fill the void of loneliness.

Just then there was a tiny mew. The kitten had found his way upstairs and was looking for company. Meg gathered him up. 'This is against the rules, my wee friend.' But she allowed him to curl up on her coverlet, and was suddenly comforted by his tiny presence. Meg slept soundly, worn out by emotion and stress.

Rory was at her gate at seven. Meg was waiting, shivering a little in the dark misty air. 'You haven't told your mother—about Grace?' she asked.

His voice was neutral as he opened the car door for her. 'No. Flora doesn't want to know the bad side of life. They're only in-laws, not sisters. I feel that Grace would be happier with just you and me.'

The morning was overcast and cold, the sea metallic grey, stretching to a drab misty sky. Even the jagged shape of the Black Rock was shrouded today, and as they neared the white shape of the Tay Bridge, the farthest piers on the Dundee side were hidden by mist. They were both preoccupied with their own thoughts. But as Rory negotiated the lights, driving on to the main Perth road where the hospital was, Meg found herself suddenly noticing the large square block of apartments where Rex Donaldson lived.

She looked sideways at Rory's profile, strong and handsome. He said quietly, 'What's on your mind, Meg?'

'Nothing. I just noticed Mr Donaldson's BMW outside his flat.'

'Dundee's answer to Casanova? I thought you were over him.'

'I am. It just brought back a few unhappy thoughts, that's all.' And Rory put his left hand over hers for a minute, in unspoken comradeship. She said rather huskily, 'You've not a bad chap when you're not shouting at me.'

'Me, shout? Never!'

Meg smiled to herself. Now was no time to argue. 'I know there are a few things on your mind.'

Rory sighed. 'Just a few. I'll be relieved when Greg gets back.' Neither of them mentioned the case of Morag Campbell, but it was uppermost in their minds, after poor Grace. Rory indicated right, and they swung round towards the large white edifice that was Ninewells Hospital. Again they lapsed into silence. They knew she had little time to go, and their thoughts mingled, with a deep and great mutual understanding. As they walked upstairs their hands touched, and they held each other's hand until they reached the ward. It made Meg feel less forlorn and alone.

Sister didn't mind them going into the small private room. Grace lay on her back, so perfectly still that for a moment Meg thought she wasn't breathing. She gave a little cry, but at the sound Grace turned her head, and a smile came to her lips, and to her pale blue eyes. A student nurse was at the foot of the bed. She nodded, and left the room, saying, 'She took half a cup of warm milk.'

Rory and Meg stood one on each side of her, taking a hand each. Outside, there was a sudden gust of wind, and the remains of the mist began to swirl away.

'Thank you for coming.' Grace's voice was weak. 'My dear children——'

Meg leaned forward. 'There's no need to talk, Auntie. The wind is getting up, and you can't compete. We just wanted to come and see you—be with you . . .'

'I haven't lost my voice, lass. But I know there's no need of empty talk with us—with the three of us.'

Meg felt her eyes wet with tears, and she saw Rory felt

the same. Grace's hand today felt cold and dry, her breathing was audible.

Grace whispered, 'Rory, have you had the hearing at the FPC yet?'

'No, Auntie. Next Monday, I'm told.'

Grace smiled at him. 'Good luck. I know it will be all right—your good name will see you through.' She took a deep breath then, as another gust of wind whooshed against the window. 'I was born in a storm.' She closed her eyes. 'I love the wind.' The two of them sat by her, listening to the music of the winds she loved, as it gusted round the hospital walls and in the tall trees nearby, and the wild waters of the River Tay, and the North Sea beyond the estuary.

Sister came in then. She looked at Grace, and felt the pulse in her thin neck. 'Let her sleep,' she advised gently.

Meg said, 'You don't want us to stay?'

'You may stay as long as you like—but I think she'll sleep for a wee while, don't you?'

It was Rory who nodded and answered, as Meg found herself unable to speak. 'She'll sleep her little life away. She'll go with the wind, the way she came. It's as she wanted.'

Meg bent and kissed the papery cheek and rested her head against it for a moment. 'Goodbye, Auntie. I'll be back later.'

She ran down the stairs to the car. Rory followed, and they sat for a while with unseeing eyes, in the front of the scarlet car. Then his voice, very strangled, said, 'Meg——' and they turned towards one another. He took her in his arms, and they held each other tightly, as though the agony might go away if they shared it. Meg felt his heart beating. This was more than the boy she had once known. This was the man she had come to love; at that moment, she felt they were one. As they embraced, in a mutual unhappiness of loss, she thought a thousand thoughts, of wild days of childhood, of wandering along

the shore to the cry of gulls, and of walking in the fields
and forests of Fife, with the wind in the trees, and with
the carefree hearts of youth. He was the big boy then,
and she was the wee girl who tagged along at the back,
and had to plead to play with him. Today it was Rory
who had turned to her for comfort. They were equals
now, joined in their grief.

He put her thoughts into words as they finally drew
apart, eyes damp but hearts more settled, soothed by
being together. 'I'm glad you were with me.'

Meg nodded. 'Grace was glad too.'

He turned to the front and took the key from his
pocket. He drew in his breath. They both knew that they
would not see Grace's blue eyes again lit with the light of
life. 'Are you ready?'

'Yes.' Her voice was low, almost unheard as Rory
switched on the engine, and the wind blustered around
the car. He had put the top up, and the draughts
somehow got in and made even more noise than the
wind outside. 'Yes, let's go.'

'She'll sleep peacefully, Meg.'

'I know.'

As they drove back along the familiar road, Meg felt
they were losing the intimacy that their shared grief had
momentarily given them. She saw Rory's thoughts turning back to the problems of the day, to getting the calls
done, and coping with the outbreak of gastric 'flu that
had hit the village, doubling his workload at a time when
Dr Gregory was still on holiday.

They went into the surgery in Harbour Lane together,
and Rory hung up his coat in the office and went straight
through to his room. The waiting room was full. He said
nothing more to Meg. She smiled at Mrs Blyth, who
asked, concerned, 'How is Miss Henderson?'

'Asleep.' Meg felt her heart turn over. 'Very
peaceful.'

'That's as it should be. She was a good woman.' And
Meg noticed that Mrs Blyth had already put Grace into

the past tense. 'I'll take the doctor a cuppie of tea—the kettle's boiled. You'll take one too, Meg?'

Meg nodded. 'Rory once asked me why I wasted my training in a small town. I think he knows why now.'

'There now, don't you fret, Meg Mackenzie.' The older woman was kindly. 'It must be hard on you too, your father being only a month back from Ninewells too. Can't you get someone else from the council to take over from you this morning? You shouldn't have to work.'

'I'm better working, Mrs Blyth, thanks. I like to be busy.'

'I'll away and take the doctor his tea, then.'

Meg went off to do her regular visits, glad to see the familiar faces, and conscious of the goodwill they all felt for her. She realised that Jessie would very soon be back to take over—and she would be out of a job. She drove back from Nethergate Grange, knowing that the big empty house was waiting—and she felt very alone. Even Catriona would not be there. And very soon the house itself would be sold, and she would have to find somewhere to live.

She arrived back at the surgery feeling numb. Rory had just finished seeing patients, and Meg looked up hopefully, waiting for a kindly word or a gesture that showed he still understood her, shared her thoughts. But Rory said nothing apart from discussing patients. It was as though he felt he had been too emotional that morning, that he had shown too much weakness. He had retreated behind honest Scottish restraint and dislike of too much open show of grief. She waited for something—just a word, a sign, but he collected his calls, put on his coat, and picked up his bag. 'Well, ladies, I'll be off,' he said.

''Bye, Doctor.'

Meg swallowed, unable to say anything. Rory's keen blue eyes looked at her for just one second, before looking back at his list of calls. 'Try and get some rest,

Meg,' he said. She nodded briefly. At least he had said something. If he had left her that morning, she felt so completely alone she would have collapsed in tears. At least he had noticed her . . .

Craigie House looked extra large, as she parked her small car at the side and let herself in through the massive front door. Her footsteps echoed down the hall. Suddenly a small ball of black fur came tottering out of the kitchen towards her. The kitten! She bent and swept the tiny form up to her chest and hugged it. 'Hello, my wee friend. You're so huge that I'm going to call you Alexander the Great.' And she kissed the top of its little head, vibrating as it was with purring. It was amazing that this scrap of fur made the whole house seem full again, yet he was so small that he could get lost in the shadows.

Meg had to go to the kitchen to feed the cat, so she automatically made herself a coffee, and took a cream cracker and a piece of cheese through to the drawing room. The rain was just beginning—great blobs of water hitting the windows as though thrown from buckets. She tried to carry on as normal, lighting the log fire in the drawing room, to try and cheer the place up. The grandfather clock, that had once sounded so merry, now chimed sonorously, its voice melancholy as it struck four. As the last echo died away, the telephone rang. She knew it would be the hospital. 'She just slipped away with a sigh. Yes, I've notified Dr Henderson. He's making the necessary arrangements.'

She sat in the hall for a while, listening to the rain and the wind. It was dark, but she knew the number of Dr Gregory's, where Rory was living, and she dialled it with hands that felt weak and listless. There was no human answer; the machine merely gave the number, said that the doctor was out, and asked her to try again in half an hour. The voice on the machine was Rory's, but it sounded impersonal—certainly not the voice of the warm tender man who had embraced her that morning.

Meg sat with the kitten on her lap, until her hands felt cold, and she went through and sat by the flickering fire without putting the light on.

There was a ring at the bell. Rory! With lighter heart, she got up, and put Alexander on the rug while she ran down to the door. She flung it open—but it was Alistair, dripping wet, his collar turned up, his hair plastered to his head.

'Oh, Alistair—come away in, won't you?'

She tried to hide her disappointment, and welcome him. It was kind of him to come, but she hoped he wouldn't try and comfort her. There was nothing anyone could do. But Alistair said nothing about Grace. 'Meg —' and his voice was taut with worry, 'Murdoch's boat is missing. It didn't come back this morning.'

'Oh no!' she gasped. 'Is his brother with him? Young Alan?'

'Yes. They're both experienced—they know these shores from childhood, I know. But they got separated from the others, and there's been no radio contact.'

'Will they launch the lifeboat?'

'I believe so.' His face was lined with the anxiety. 'I've just tried Rory's number, but there's no reply, and Dr Ross is busy in Anstruther. Do you think you could bring a medical kit down to the harbour? Just in case?'

'Of course. It's in the surgery—I'll get the key.' Meg had changed into trousers earlier, and now she took an extra sweater and an anorak with a hood against the weather. She locked the door, leaving the hall light on. 'It looks more homely to come home to,' she explained.

'How is Grace?' Alistair asked her.

Meg stopped at the gate, the rain lashing her face. 'You haven't heard?'

He faced her then, and took her into his arms. 'I'm so sorry.'

'We have work to do, Alstair,' she reminded him.

'I wish I didn't have to ask you, but I feel we ought to have someone with medical knowledge.'

'I'm glad to help.' She led the way down Harbour Lane, and took Jessie's bag from the surgery. 'Let's hope I'm not needed.'

'Rory must be at the hospital, then?'

'Or with his mother. He'll be here as soon as he can, I'm sure.' They walked down to the harbour wall, where several ex-fishermen stood around under cover of the boat sheds, peering anxiously at the horizon. They were used to such weather and ignored the driving rain. Murdoch McLeod wasn't married, and his mother was dead. His father had gone to live with his married sister in Aberdeen, so there was no one from his own family to stand and watch and wait. But the whole village was a family at times like this; they all lived each other's sorrows, as well as their joys.

Hamish Robertson and Donnie McCallum had gone out with Murdoch last night, but they had made it back before the storm got too bad, and now they stood, huddled in their oilskins, their hands clenched tightly, waiting for some sighting, some news from their comrade. Meg went up to Hamish. Shouting in the teeth of the gale, she said, 'What would you have done?'

'Made for Elie,' he shouted back. 'Not so many rocks, if you're being tossed about.' He pointed out to sea. 'He'll be better to ride out the storm, not make for harbour. Too many rocks along this shore.'

'He'll know that well enough?'

'Aye, he kens it. If he has control, that is.'

There was a hoarse shout. 'There—a boat!'

'Looks as though he's drifting!'

Hamish said, 'If he's no engine, he'll hit the rocks. I'm going out.'

Sam Hamilton, the harbourmaster, said, 'Nay, wait and see.'

'Let me have the launch, Sam. I'll need to get a line on board. Donnie'll come along. They might be injured, though.' Hamish looked at Meg.

'Give me a lifejacket.' She wasn't going to let them go

without her if someone was hurt. 'I've got splints and bandages. Let's go, Hamish.' And she struggled into the lifejacket that was handed to her, wrapping a tape round the handle of the medical bag, so that it was attached to her wrist even if she lost hold of it.

'Good lassie!' Hamish used to sit by Meg in school. He knew she could do what any boy could do—and if she couldn't she was always determined to do it none the less. 'Come away down, and let me fasten the rope to this rail.' Safely attached to the launch, the three friends cast off from the sheltered harbour and made for the tossing, bobbing toy out there in the open sea.

As soon as they were within hailing distance, Hamish cupped his hands and gave a might shout. They waited. Then Murdoch's bare head appeared on deck. He waved, and shouted something they couldn't hear. Hamish said, 'It must be Alan.' He edged the boat closer. It would be daft to go too near and be dashed against the other craft.

Hamish said, 'The tide will be on the turn. If we wait, the wind will drop.' They switched off the engine, tossing with little control over their craft.

Meg's heart was beating fast. 'Ask him where Alan is,' she said.

Hamish looked across. Murdoch's figure was on deck now, clearly seen moving about, but there was no sign of his brother. Hamish shouted, 'How's Alan?'

And amid the roar of the waves, they heard, 'His arm. Broken, I think.'

Meg could cope with that. 'When can you get alongside?'

'I'll try in ten minutes. Look, the tide is on the turn—see how it swells and subsides without making breakers. Patience, lass, I dinna want more than one casualty!'

The minutes passed agonisingly slowly. But then Hamish started the engine. 'Right, Meg, get ready. I'll try and get alongside, but I'll keep hold of the lifeline, so

Free Books Certificate

Dear Susan,

Please send me my 4 free Doctor Nurse Romances together with my free clock. Please also reserve a special Reader Service subscription for me. If I decide to subscribe, I shall receive 6 superb new titles every two months for just £7.20, post and packing free. If I decide not to subscribe, I shall write to you within 10 days. The free books and clock will be mine to keep in any case.

I understand that I am under no obligation whatsoever — I can cancel my subscription at any time simply by writing to you. I am over 18 years of age.

Your FREE
Digital Quartz
Desk Clock

Name: _____
(BLOCK CAPITALS PLEASE)

Address: _____

_____

_____ Postode _____

Signature _____

〔logo〕 5A8D

The right is reserved to refuse an application and change the terms of this offer. You may be mailed with other offers as a result of this application. Offer expires December 31st 1988. Overseas send for details.

To Susan Welland
Mills & Boon Reader Service
FREEPOST
Croydon
Surrey
CR9 9EL

SEND NO MONEY NOW

dinna you fear to jump when I tell you.' Gradually he edged the small boat with consummate skill nearer to the small trawler. Murdoch was waiting, keeping his own boat as level as possible. Then Hamish shouted, 'Now!' and Meg pushed off from the side of the launch straight at Murdoch McLeod, who grabbed her as she landed and pulled the line clear.

'Well done, Meggie!' He pointed to the deck, where he had tried to make Alan comfortable with his head on a coil of rope, and spare oilskins wedging him as still as possible on the tossing deck. Meg knelt at his side, pulling the medical bag round from where it had been lashed to her body.

'It isn't broken, Murdoch, he's dislocated it. Come away over here and help me.'

'Can you do it?' Alan was lying, his face contorted with pain, his eyes tightly closed.

'I'll try. The longer it stays dislocated, the worse it will be.' She looked across the injured body into Murdoch's face. 'He'll shout, Murdoch—it's painful. But once it's back the pain will ease, OK?'

'Just tell me what to do, lass.'

Murdoch's face was grim, as he watched Meg take the affected arm and tie it with a bandage into a flexed position. She said urgently, 'Now, this must work, Murdoch, so I'll need all your strength to push when I tell you.' The man nodded. Meg put Murdoch's hands on the arm of his brother, and slowly rotated it to the front of his body. Then she lifted it to the side. Alan groaned, but Meg said nothing, until she had rotated it as far as she could. 'Now, Murdoch! Push now!' She held the joint in the correct place, though she knew her own strength was not enough. But Murdoch pushed as she guided the limb. They forgot the rolling of the boat, the whistling of the wind in the rigging. Alan screamed, then bit his lip, and moaned. Suddenly the shoulder slipped into place. Meg wrapped it against his body, with Murdoch helping. She said, 'Get us to shore, Murdoch.

He'll be all right now.' And she sat beside the patient,
her own face sweating as his was.

The rest of the rescue was a blur to Meg. They came
into harbour, towed by the launch, and tied up in the
usual berth. Willing hands passed down a stretcher, and
Alan was lifted to the waiting ambulance. Meg and
Murdoch untied their lifelines, amid cheers and shouts
of relief from those on shore. The rain had eased, as they
thought it might at the turn of the tide. It was getting
dark, but the harbour lights were on, and mugs of hot tea
were thrust into their hands as they climbed on the damp
stones of the harbour.

Then Meg felt a strong arm around her, and she
looked up to see Rory, his eyes tragic. Behind him was
Alistair, but Rory shouldered him aside. 'I'll get her
home,' he muttered, and the minister backed away,
seeing that she needed medical rather than spiritual
support just then. But she saw the look in his eyes, and in
spite of her weariness she felt a surge of pity for him.
Rory lifted her bodily into his car and drove her to
Craigie House, where he opened the door with her key
and carried her inside, placing her on the sofa where
Grace had spent so many hours. The fire was dying, and
Rory went over to shake out the wood ash and put
another log. Meg lay still for a while, still in her outer
clothes, and gradually her heartbeats settled down, and
she felt recovered enough to pull off the anorak and her
top sweater, leaning back against the cushions, feeling
too weary to do anything but drop them on the floor
beside her.

She bent to take off her boots, but suddenly Rory was
there doing it for her. 'Lie back, lass. Where does Grace
keep the brandy?'

'Kitchen cupboard. But I don't need . . .' He had
already gone to fetch it, and when he came back he
carried a mug of warm milk, honey and brandy, which
Meg sipped slowly, while he sat beside her. She said,
'I'm all right, Rory, honestly.'

'I should have been there.'

'You can't be everywhere,' she pointed out.

'You shouldn't have had to go.' He seemed to be punishing himself, and Meg was too tired to argue with him. She leaned back against the cushions, warm and comfortable—and suddenly very, very tired. The fire flickered, sending shadows on the walls. Rory drew the curtains. She knew he was in the room, but she was unable to keep her eyes open any more, or care what went on around her.

CHAPTER SEVEN

WHEN SHE woke, Meg was unsure for a moment where she was. It was dark, and her limbs ached, her back ached. But somehow she felt pleased with herself—then she remembered why. She had clambered on board a crippled trawler and helped an injured man. His shoulder . . . of course—he had been taken to hospital, so he would be all right. She struggled to sit up, to rid herself of the blanket which held her so warmly, although she was still in her clothes.

'It's all right, I'm here, Meg.'

She looked over. She was in the drawing room, and Rory Henderson was stirring in the armchair, his eyes weary and his hair dishevelled. 'You stayed with me?' she queried.

He rose and went over to draw back the curtains, letting in a sweet gentle morning. 'You did my job for me.' He was blaming himself for putting her in danger.

'That's not how I see it, Rory. They needed someone who knew first aid, and I was the nearest, that's all.' Meg swung her legs to the floor. 'Oh, Rory—Grace is dead, and we haven't had a chance to mourn.' She sat looking down, suddenly despondent, empty. It wasn't even her home any more. She would have to get out, find some other place to live—perhaps go back to Father and Laurel Villa.

He came over and sat by her, and she knew that he felt the same—lost and saddened by the passing of Grace Henderson. 'She would have been glad. She never wanted us to be unhappy.' He looked down at her. She didn't turn, so he put out a hand and turned her face towards him. 'Meg, you depended too much on Grace. You must live your own life now.'

'I know.' She did know; Grace had constantly reminded her that she must think of her own career. Meg bent her head. 'You were right, Rory—I was a small-town girl.'

'I shouldn't have said that. I didn't know until I spoke to your father just how unnaturally he treated you. Under the circumstances, I should have praised you to the skies for being so normal. I'm sorry, Meg, I'm really sorry.'

It was nice to have Rory apologise. Especially as she didn't blame him for his comments anyway. It was nice to have him sitting beside her, their shoulders touching—sitting as friends. Now that Grace was gone, she realised Rory was the only other person in Brathay she felt really close to. And though it was clear he cared about her it was definite that his feelings were of friendship only, and nothing deeper, as her own were . . .

'Well, Meg, I must get back to the surgery,' said Rory. 'Patients don't wait.'

'Wait for me. I'll make coffee for us, and we can go together.'

'No, there's no need. Jessie rang last night. She's coming back to work this morning.'

Meg felt deprived suddenly. She wanted to work. 'But surely you aren't going to allow her to do a full day straight away?'

'I'll help her out. Be sensible, lass. You can't tell me you feel a hundred per cent—not after what you did yesterday?'

She nodded, regretfully. 'My back aches, but I can still work.'

'No, lass, don't let me have to plead with you. Take it easy today—try to think of nothing, and just stay on the sofa. Here, your little cat wants you to stay, doesn't he? See how he hates it when you move away?' Rory smiled into her eyes, and she had to smile back.

She tried to do as Rory prescribed. She made herself

coffee and toast, then she had a thorough shower and washed her hair. She dressed in comfortable clothes and went downstairs again, seeing the kitten looking from the sofa with its wide-eyed expression of total trust. She sat by him and stroked his head.

The bell rang. She hoped no one was going to praise her or anything embarrassing like that, but it was Caroline Forbes who stood on the front steps. 'Hello, Meg. Feeling OK today?'

'Yes, thank you. Won't you come in?'

'Just for a moment. A few words with you over a business matter.'

'Really?' Meg couldn't imagine what, but she led the way into the drawing room, and threw another log on the fire. Caroline was wearing a heather tweed suit, elegantly cut with a long-line jacket and a mink collar. Her bright gold earrings would have looked vulgar on Meg, but on the model-shaped Caroline they looked, as usual, stunning.

Caroline sat primly on the edge of the armchair seat. 'Meg dear, I won't waste your time. You must want to rest, after the day you had yesterday. I just want to offer you a fair price for Craigie House. I do own some property round here, as you know, and we wouldn't want people from outside the village to buy into our little community, now would we?'

'Craigie House?' Meg was taken aback. 'It doesn't belong to me. I have no idea who Auntie has left it to.'

'Oh, my dear, she never told you? Oh, I do hope I haven't put my foot in it, dear. She's left Craigie House to you and Rory jointly. You didn't know? Then I bring you good news, don't I?'

'I suppose you do.' But Meg's head was reeling suddenly. How on earth had Caroline found out about Grace's will? There was only one person who could have told her—Rory Henderson. And as he was too tactful to offer to buy himself, Caroline was doing it for him. How deceitful and underhand! Meg felt a growing rage inside her, and her stubbornness came to the fore, as it always did when she was surprised. In a steely voice she said, 'This is news to me. I had no idea. But if what you say is true, then I shall have to make my own plans. I may even buy Rory's half and stay here. It's much too soon to make up my mind, Caroline. So perhaps you'd have the decency to wait at least until after the funeral before making commercial propostions, OK?' And she stood up and opened the drawing room door, so that Caroline had no option but to leave.

At the door the other woman said, 'Think it over carefully, Meg. Outside developers will turn this place into a hotel at best, and at worst holiday flatlets. I've quite a few contacts, and that's what I've heard. Think it over, and let me know what you decide. It will be best for Brathay—and for all of us.' She smiled brilliantly and walked away on her patent leather boots—the sea sparkled behind her, innocent of the contriving and the decent that exuded from her at that moment.

Anger was Meg's only emotion. She walked back to the fire and made it up carefully. She left some milk and some food for the kitten. Then she took her coat from the hall and went out to the car. She didn't know where she was going, but she had to think. Craigie House —half hers. And already Rory was plotting through Caroline to buy the whole place. Why hadn't he mentioned it himself? She might even have agreed. After all, it was far too big for Meg alone. She probably couldn't afford to heat the place, in spite of her father's gifts. She sat in the car for a while, waiting for her annoyance to calm down. Then she switched on the engine and drove out on to the coast road. Yes, if Rory had been open with her, she might have agreed. But now—she set her lips in a grim line. Craigie was half hers, and she would hang on to it for as long as it took. She would get a job, and even buy him out, if she had to. She put her foot down, and the old car fairly raced along towards St Andrews.

It was term time, and the students were all about the

old grey town in their warm red gowns, not just for show, but as an extra barrier against the cold east wind. Meg went into a health food shop in Fishergate and ordered home-made soup and a wholemeal roll. It was almost lunchtime, and she found that anger made her hungry.

She sat over the soup, conflicting memories in her mind—some of sunny happy days with Rory and the other kids. Some sad ones, as she realised how much Caroline Forbes was in his confidence. She wished she had not allowed herself to love him; it made today's shock all the more painful.

'Why, if it isn't Meg Mackenzie, but all that's wonderful!'

She heard the words, but for a moment she thought she was imagining them. But when a masculine figure sat down opposite to her, she dragged her thoughts back to the present. The masculine form was handsome and smiling, and though the last time she had seen Rex Donaldson she had vowed never to speak to him again —well, today things were different. 'What a surprise, Rex! How are you? And what are you doing in St Andrews?'

'Came to give a lecture to the Medical Society.' He ordered coffee. 'Meg, you look lovely. Why are you here?'

'I—just came out—to be by myself for a while.'

'Do you want me to leave?'

'No, no. I've—well, I'm just out of work at the moment, and I was trying to decide what to do with my life. My—my aunt died recently, and I've no dependants. I'm my own boss now. Father is well—doesn't need me.'

Rex's eyes were brown and very expressive. Meg remembered when she was head over heels in love with him—how she hung on his every word. She smiled, and he said, 'That's a knowing smile, Meg. So you're pleased to see me, then?'

'Yes.' Her anger forgotten, she rejoiced that Rex no

longer had any power over her heart. 'I'm pleased to say that I know you for what you are now—and under those circumstances, it's very nice to see you again. And of course, I'm grateful for what you did for Father.'

Rex sipped his coffee, without taking his eyes from her, while she watched him, unabashed by his attention. He put his cup down. 'Meg Mackenzie, you have the most wicked gleam in your eye!' He leaned across and whispered, 'Come and work with me, my dear. The Sister I have now is an old trout.'

She looked down modestly. 'In fact, I have been considering Ninewells. My friend Lindsay McDonald still works there, and she's always telling me there's no better place.'

Rex smoothed back his crinkly brown hair. Meg tried to forget how it had felt when she first touched it. His eyes were serious. 'Come to think of it, there's going to be a vacancy in Intensive Care after Christmas. Sister Knowles is giving up for a stint in Saudi Arabia.'

They talked. The atmosphere was light and totally pleasing. They ordered more coffee, joked about past colleagues and present difficulties. Meg began to realise just how potent was Rex's charm—he genuinely cared. Yet he had that streak of selfishness that helped him to escape from any genuine attachment. And that day, Meg knew she felt the same. She didn't want to belong. She didn't want to be obliged to anyone. She was her own boss. The end had come for anyone who tried to manipulate her. She felt powerful, and strong, and she realised her own worth—that was important.

She began to think it was time to go, and looked at her watch. 'Rex, do you realise how long we've been here?'

He looked too. 'Meg, you fascinating creature, I had no idea. It's nearly dinnertime. How about you and me having dinner? After all, you only had a bowl of soup for lunch.'

'And a dozen coffees?' Meg laughed. 'If you don't have to get back to Dundee, I'll buy you dinner. After all, you bought me a few, way back in the old days.'

'No—I insist. Just this once, Meg? Dinner at the Old Course?'

'I couldn't,' she protested. 'Not in these clothes.'

'You look wonderful,' Rex assured her.

And so the evening ended with a most unexpected meal at the best hotel in town. And Meg enjoyed it enormously. She knew why—she had met Rex at a time when they both felt the same. For once she shared his dislike of permanent promises. For once she was as sceptical as he of any lasting relationship. And for once she knew she was capable of keeping him at arm's length.

He walked with her to her car, and she didn't object when he put his arm around her. She said, 'I'm going to be busy for a while—lots to clear up, and Aunt Grace's will has to be seen to. I might even leave town.'

They exchanged a smile, as Rex murmured, 'I'll be in touch long before that, darling.'

She drove back to Brathay in a very different frame of mind than when she had arrived in St Andrews. The memory of Rory was still bitter-sweet, but now it seemed a long time ago that she was helplessly in love with her childhood hero. The pain was there—but it was in the past too, and she felt confident that it would pass . . . Dear Rory! He was a beloved part of her old life. With the help of Caroline and Rex, tomorrow she could start building a new life. A life based on reality—on things as they were, not as she dreamed them to be.

It was very dark as she opened the front door of Craigie House. Alexander came trotting out to meet her, and she gathered him up in her arms. The fire had just about gone out, with only a faint glow among the embers. Meg held the purring creature to her as she went round drawing the curtains. The agony of Caroline's words had faded and Meg was in charge now. She was pleased to be in touch with Rex again—and pleased that he was anxious to see her again. She had put him off—something she never had the guts to in the past. And she could tell by the look in his face that he wanted very much to see her again.

The telephone shrilled in the darkness, and she put the kitten down to answer it. 'Hello?' Her voice reflected her optimism, her new-found self-confidence.

'Meg Mackenzie, where have you been? I've been worried sick!'

It was Rory. Meg exulted in being able to say, 'No need, Rory Henderson. I can look after myself, and I've no need to tell folks where I go.'

His voice changed, almost apologetic, in fact. He said, 'I deserved that. But I've been trying to get you for quite a while.'

'I met a friend,' she told him.

'A boyfriend?'

'Does it matter?'

'I'm sorry.' He paused. 'About tomorrow . . .'

Meg's conscience smote her. 'Your hearing, Rory! I'll be there. If they need my testimony, they can jolly well have it.'

'May I—come and talk about it?' he asked tentatively.

'Now?'

'Yes—if you don't mind?'

Meg smiled in the darkness. 'You've always been welcome, Rory. We have no secrets from each other.' Except that he gets his girlfriend to offer to buy my house, she thought grimly. But Rory's FPC hearing was tomorrow, and as a loyal friend she must help him over that.

The drawing room fire was out now, but the kitchen one was still alight, damped down as it was to keep the central heating going. Meg went, though, and poked it, coaxing some flickering flames before she put the kettle on. Alexander followed her, and she gave him another sardine while she waited for Rory.

Rory came in without speaking. He took his anorak

off in the kitchen and hung it on the back of the chair. In spite of her new independence, Meg's heart went out to him. 'The kettle's on, Rory. And what I told Dr Whyte I saw, I fully intend to swear to.'

'You shouldn't have said it in the first place,' he told her.

'But I know you so well that I can quite happily swear that you did no wrong.'

The kitten jumped up into Rory's lap and he caressed the small head before looking up at Meg. 'Thanks.' A muscle tensed in his jaw, and she saw tenderness in his eyes. He caught her hand in his and kissed her fingers. He said hoarsely, 'I'd better go.' And as he stood, and the kitten leapt down reluctantly, Rory turned and caught Meg into his embrace, finding her lips with his, holding them for a long time.

Meg's resolve was suddenly in tatters. She went to the door with him, their arms about each other. His arm slid down, but he still seemed to want to hold on to her, and their hands gripped before he turned and ran down the steps. She watched him go. He was on foot, and she listened for his footsteps until they disappeared.

Then there was nothing but the sound of the waves, constantly lapping at the shore. Meg stood gazing where Rory had been. Tomorrow he would be facing a tribunal which could ruin his professional life. She thought of Grace's last words—'Your good character will see you through,' she had thought. But surely Meg should be doing more? She went back to the hallway, put the light on, and checked through the phone book. Campbell. There were many, but Meg persevered.

'Hello? Is that Morag? Meg Mackenzie here.'

There was a pause. 'What do you want?'

'I thought I'd just remind you that an innocent person has to go and prove his innocence tomorrow at eleven. Can you live with that, Morag?'

'It's none of your business!' snapped Morag.

'Honour is everyone's business. Morag, this will harm

you for the rest of your life. It can't harm Dr Henderson, his name is too well known; the other doctors won't believe bad things about him. Don't forget, you have no good name to live up to. Tomorrow is a good time to start.'

The phone was slammed down. Meg sighed, and replaced her receiver. There was nothing else she could do now, so she went slowly upstairs. It had been a busy day and she slept soundly, after a final prayer for justice for Rory.

Next morning Meg was waiting at the window. She saw Rory's red car streak past the house. He must have done his calls quickly. She imagined how his heart must be beating at the injustice of this whole affair. She watched long after the roar of his engine had faded, and decided suddenly that she had to be there, even though Dr Whyte had not contacted her to give evidence. She ought to support Rory. Even if she just faced Morag, her very presence might help to move the child's conscience.

The hearing was at St Andrews; Meg drove the familiar road, down past Crail. The lifeboat station was quiet today, the sea gentle and bright in the sun. She drew up outside the FPC offices in North Street. The scarlet sports car was there, strangely sad without its owner. Meg parked close to him and walked slowly up the steps, but she almost collided with Rory himself, running down the steps as though in a hurry to get away.

'Rory, what happened?' she asked anxiously.

'Postponed. Decision this afternoon.'

They stood facing each other. 'It was sweet of you to come,' Rory said at last.

'I didn't think they'd take so long to decide. It seems so very obvious Morag is lying.' Meg looked up at him. 'Rory, I know a place where the home-made soup is delicious.'

He gave a half smile, and her heart moved at the tension in his familiar kind face. 'If you hadn't been here, I'd have settled for a pint.' He took her hand and

tucked it into the crook of his arm. 'Come away, Meg
Mackenzie. We'll try the soup.'

Over the meal, he said, 'Let's talk about you, Meg.
Will you be looking for another job? If you want to stay
with the practice, Dr Gregory would be happy to take
you on, you know.'

'I'm going back to hospital work—ICU. There's a job
going at Ninewells.' She was too gentle to tell him that it
was Caroline's insensitive offer to buy her out of Craigie
House. Let Rory's case be over before she gave him any
more hassle.

'Don't you want to stay in Brathay?' he asked.

'When I want advice, I'll ask for it!' Meg was suddenly
angry.

'Sorry,' he apologised.

'No, I'm sorry. You must be nervous, waiting for this
thing to be over.'

Rory looked at his watch. 'Yes, in a way. Thanks for
keeping me company.' He pushed away his unfinished
coffee. 'I'd better be getting back.'

'I'll come with you,' said Meg.

'You sure?'

'Of course.'

'I don't want you to testify,' he persisted.

Meg smiled. 'Oh, Rory, don't worry about me.
You've got quite enough to think about—your patients,
arranging the funeral, coping with Mrs Campbell
and her hysterical daughter . . . I won't add to your
problems. Let's go and face the music.'

He stood up and helped her on with her coat. As they
went out into the cool wind, he said, 'There's one more
worry you didn't mention.'

'What's that?'

'You haven't told me who you were with yesterday.'

Meg was flattered. 'In the middle of a trial you think of
that?'

Rory waited on the pavement. 'Are you going to tell
me?'

She relented. 'It was only Rex. Now let's get back.'

They started to walk together. Rory said quietly, 'Are you sure that's wise?'

'Seeing Rex? It's my business, Rory.'

'Yes. Yes, of course it is. Sorry.' And they walked the rest of the way in silence. But outside the offices of the Family Practitioner Committee Mrs Campbell was waiting with Morag. Rory and Meg stopped short, but it was too late.

'I knew Meg Mackenzie couldn't give evidence. Just look at her—she's soft on him—it's plain as anything!' Mrs Campbell's face was distorted with triumph. She grabbed the girl and stalked into the doorway. Rory looked at Meg, and she was moved by the sincerity in his eyes.

Just then Dr Whyte appeared, on his way from lunch. 'Ah, good afternoon, Dr Henderson, come away in. My colleagues will be there by now.' Rory followed him, standing back politely for his senior to precede him into the building. Meg didn't go in, but turned and wandered along the street, looking into shop windows but seeing nothing. She dabbed briefly at her eyes. Poor Rory! She couldn't help caring for him. Waiting was the hardest part.

She was conscious that someone was standing beside her, and she turned, wiping her eyes again. 'Morag!' she exclaimed. 'What are you doing here?'

'The committee—they're talking things over.'

Meg said nothing, but Morag knew what she thought. The girl said, 'Why are you no mad at me?'

Meg took a deep breath and turned to the girl. 'Screaming at you won't help, Morag. You know right from wrong, and you're choosing to lie. What can I do to stop you?'

Morag looked down, and nibbled at a fingernail. Then in a very low voice she said, 'Will you come with me? I'll tell them Geoff did it.'

'You'll—what? Confess?'

'Aye. I wanted to this morning, but Mother wouldna listen.'

Meg held out her hand and the girl shook it. Then they walked back into the building. Mrs Campbell was sitting on a chair in the corridor. Morag walked straight past her and knocked at a door. Her mother stared, then tried to pull her back, but Morag shook her off and went into the room. The door was ajar, and they could hear her voice—clear and slightly shaky. 'I'm sorry for all the fuss. It wasna him, it was my boyfriend. I lied because my mother would have killed me.'

A man's voice, polite and genteel. 'Do you swear that, Miss Campbell?'

'Aye, I do.'

'You've caused a great deal of disruption—wasted a lot of people's time.'

'Aye, I ken.'

'And you are aware Dr Henderson might have lost his job?'

'I never meant for it to go this far.' Morag was near to tears. The gentle voice told her to run along, and remember always to be honest in future.

Then Rory spoke, Meg's heart warmed to him as he was totally forgiving. 'Just apologise to the committee for wasting their time, Morag. I understand you feared your mother's anger.'

'Aye, I did. And she made me keep saying it. She said Miss Mackenzie was sweet on the doctor, so no one would believe she saw anything.'

Meg's face went hot, and Mrs Campbell seemed struck dumb. She shot a venomous glance at Meg, and Meg decided that she was no longer needed. Rory was cleared; that was all that mattered. She walked out of the building and across North Street, past Rory's scarlet car; but he wouldn't need her now. She felt a great weight lift from her as she walked, and she felt an admiration for the girl who had, in the face of her mother's wrath, taken the right decision.

She drove back quickly, as she wanted to let Alistair know that all was well. But as she neared Craigie House, she noticed a car parked in the drive, and as she drew up outside, she saw the familiar figure of Rex Donaldson, tall and slim in his expensive camel coat. His face brightened as he spotted her. 'Meg, my dear, thank goodness! Now we can have dinner together.'

'Not tonight, Rex,' she apologised. 'I feel like a damp rag.'

He took her lightly in his arms. 'I have the perfect antidote to that.'

'No, Rex.' She moved his arms away. 'It isn't like last time. I really mean it: I don't want to go out with you, except as a friend. And I know that isn't the way you like to play things. Go back to Dundee, Rex. You're a long way from home, and there's no one in Brathay who'll come out and play.'

His broad smile showed that he was by no means put off. 'Angel, that's exactly the way I want to play things. Let's relax together—no hanky-panky, promise.'

Meg couldn't help laughing at his bounciness. 'Mr Donaldson, I happen to know you! The leopard that couldn't change his spots if he tried! Forget it. Go and find some innocent young student nurse who'll fall at your feet.'

Rex tried the sincere approach. 'I'd rather have the prettiest woman in Fife. Honestly, Meg.' He pointed to the silver BMW. 'Look, a luxury car and a warm and sincere human being waiting to give you a wonderful evening.'

They were laughing together now, and he had a hand on her shoulder as a red sports car appeared along the coast road and drew up with a screech of brakes at Meg's gate. Rory put the window down and stuck his head out. His look was frosty. 'I just wanted to thank you, Meg. I hoped we could have supper together, but I see you're otherwise engaged.'

'No, I'm not,' she assured him.

Rex said swiftly, 'Oh yes, you are. Evening, Rory old man.'

'Good evening, *old man!*' Rory emphasised the term. 'Oh well, must rush—Caroline will be waiting.' And with a wave that was supposed to be genial to them both, he drove off to Brathay. Meg stood and watched him. She was very sorry he hadn't waited for her, but she felt a frisson of excitement that he should appear so very angry, seeing her with Rex . . .

CHAPTER EIGHT

SHE HAD managed to get rid of Rex. It hadn't been easy, but when she told him about Grace, his finer feelings prevailed, and he left her in peace. Meg had been grateful for the evening to herself. The past days had been like a nightmare, with the death of Grace and the saving of Alan McLeod in the storm—followed straight-away by Rory's FPC hearing. Thank goodness to have weathered that one! She sat down in the kitchen armchair, her limbs aching and weary.

Someone rang the doorbell. Summoning her strength, Meg went to answer it. The gentle minister stood there, and Meg felt guilty for not ringing him earlier. 'Alistair, it's all right—Morag confessed,' she began. 'It's all over, and I'm sorry I——'

'Don't. I can see you're all in, Meg. I won't stay.'

'You're the only person I could stand just now,' she assured him.

He smiled. 'Just two things, lass. The first is the funeral. Is there anything special you want said or sung? For Grace?'

'Come and sit down, Alistair.' She led the way to the kitchen. 'There's nothing I want. Rory and Flora should decide the service.'

'They've told me enough. They asked me to speak to you.'

Meg sighed deeply. 'Alistair Reid, if anyone in this town understood what Grace Henderson meant to us all, it's you. You will say it, I know—you'll say it just as she would have wished.'

He said quietly, 'You pay me a great compliment, Meg. But will you choose a reading for me?'

'Not a reading. But if you would ask Mr Millar to play

the *Eriskay Love Lilt*? We both loved that . . .' Tears spilled over suddenly. *By love's light my foot finds its own pathway to thee . . .*

The young minister watched her for a moment, then came across and put his arms round her awkwardly at first, then more confidently. He bent and kissed her cheek. He didn't tell her to stop crying, but let her cry, after a while she was all right. 'Thank you, Alistair.' She blew her nose.

'I'll make sure we play that for you,' he promised.

'What was the other thing you came for?' Meg asked.

'Well—' Alistair seemed awkward, 'I joined the squash club, you know. I told you I was going to.'

She remembered. He had joined because of her. 'And I haven't been since then, because of working for Rory.'

'I noticed that.' His smiled was genuine, forgiving. 'As you know, Miles Thackeray is a member.'

'Oh, I'm mortified! The pantomime—Miles's pantomime!' Meg exclaimed. 'I always help. I'd completely forgotten.'

'It isn't too late or anything. He just wants to know if you'll help backstage. He needs someone experienced to do Cinderella's make-up.'

'I'd love to.' Meg sat for a while, recalling past Christmases. 'I'm not sure what I'll be doing. Grace always invited people back after the show . . . But that doesn't matter—tell him I'll help, and be glad to.'

'Good.' Alistair stood up. 'Well, Meg, I'll see you at the funeral.'

'Won't you have some coffee?' she invited.

'No, thank you. You see, I'm—fond of you. I shouldn't stay, really—I know you don't feel the same.'

They walked to the door together, and Meg felt a great sadness because Alistair loved her, and she loved Rory—and neither of them would get their heart's desire. She murmured, 'We succeeded with Morag, Alistair. She confessed this afternoon, without any more prompting from me.'

The young minister's face lit up. 'Meg, that's wonderful news! I feel like a winner for God. That news has made my day. To think she chose truth instead of lies—I'm truly grateful. My prayers have been answered—of course, I'm glad for Rory too. But for Morag, it was so important for her to take this step.'

'I know. And thank you for coming with me to Jimmy Stewart's. Mission accomplished, eh, Alistair?'

He was still smiling as he went down the path. 'Actually, I've become rather addicted to cappuccino coffee!'

In a couple of days Meg had the expected call from the solicitors, Caird and Caplan. Mr Caird himself came round to explain exactly where she stood according to Grace's will. 'You and Dr Henderson have complete ownership,' he told her. 'I'll be happy to act for either of you if you decide to transfer one half to the other.'

Meg said firmly, 'I don't want to be rushed into anything. I presume Dr Henderson feels the same. I imagine he won't want me thrown out of my half?'

Mr Caird was fatherly, though businesslike. 'I'm sure he won't, lassie. Now is there anything else I can help you with?'

She shook her head. 'I know Craigie House will have to be sold: I've come to terms with that. I just hope the town doesn't change too much.' She looked across at the white-haired solicitor, sipping the mocha coffee she had made him. 'I hear Mrs Forbes is buying up the place ready for redevelopment?'

He smiled. 'She has some property, yes, and work has already started on the fishermen's cottage in Harbour Lane. But I hardly think the character of Brathay will be altered. The renovations are extremely tasteful and discreet.'

'So no fairgrounds or Disneylands in Brathay, you think?'

'I'm almost certain.'

Meg nodded, not entirely convinced. 'I suppose the extra building work will bring more jobs to the village.'

'And the marina near Anstruther. I hear that young man you went to help—young Alan McLeod—has left fishing to go and work at the marina. Not so dangerous, yet still working with the sea he loves.'

She was glad to hear that. She hadn't seen Alan since he came out of hospital, but Rory had told her the shoulder was fine, and her reduction of the dislocation had been praised by the orthopaedic surgeons.

Then it was the day of the funeral, and Rory had called for her so that the cortège could leave from Flora's house. He was subdued, handsome in a dark grey three-piece suit. 'By rights you should walk after the coffin, Meg,' he said. 'I wanted it. But as Mother and I are related to Grace, apparently you must walk after us. I don't like it, but she insists.'

'I don't mind walking alone. She'll know I'm close.' Meg's lip trembled. 'That's all that matters.'

He turned the car into Iona Villa, the dour home of Rory's mother Flora. The coffin lay in the front room, absolutely hidden by flowers. Meg walked in quietly, kissed Flora, and went to sit in a far corner of the cold parlour. Friends like Miss MacFarlane spoke to her in hushed tones. But the atmosphere was heavy with grief.

Caroline Forbes came to sit by her, resplendent in a sable coat. To Meg's surprise, Caroline's eys were red, and her mascara had run. It made her more human, and Meg took her hand in an impulsive gesture of friendship. Rory came over to them both, and put a hand on each woman's shoulder. 'It won't be easy. You'll come back here, won't you? I can't stay, I have to get back to the surgery.'

'Isn't Greg back today?' Caroline looked up into his face.

'Yes, but later. He said he'll try to get here in time for the service.'

Caroline said, 'Well, I'll be at the bungalow when you want me.' Meg looked away. She tried to quell the suspicion, but she wondered if they were going to talk business. Mr Caird was there too—perhaps he was going to the bungalow too?

Alistair gave his usual simple but powerful performance, leading the service with tact and compassion, not allowing too much sentiment to creep in, knowing that Grace would live on in all their hearts. As they filed out to the churchyard, Mr Millar played the Hebridean music Meg had requested, and those who had not wept in the kirk wept then.

Back at the villa, Flora presided over wine and sandwiches. Meg stayed just long enough to speak to most people there, then she slipped away, back to the grave, where the mound of earth was covered with flowers till they spilled over the other plots.

'Meg Mackenzie, don't grieve, lass, don't grieve. This day would have come three years before without you. No one has done more.' Rex Donaldson came out of the shadows of the cypresses to stand beside her and put a strong arm around her shoulders. 'I've been talking to the landlord at the Fish. Everyone knows how wonderful you've been to her.'

Meg shook her head. 'Don't you see? It was I who needed her. She filled such a gaping hole in my life. And now I've got no one.'

'That's why I'm here.' His arm was tight about her. 'I'm not trying a line, Meg. I just knew you'd need someone, that's all.'

And he lived up to his word, staying with her as long as she wanted to stay by Grace's grave, then walking back with her, expecting no conversation, just holding her, comforting her, stroking her hair.

They went into Craigie House, and Rex went through to the kitchen and put on the kettle. Meg heard voices, and went through after him into the kitchen. There was Catriona, her eyes bloated and red with weeping, sitting by the fire, and asking Rex Donaldson what he was doing in her kitchen. Meg went to her without a word, and held her tight. Caddy, more than anyone, perhaps, had been grateful to Grace Henderson. 'Please let me stay for a while? I'm no feeling so well, and I feel at home here.'

'Stay as long as you like Caddy,' Meg said gently.

'Will I be making you some broth?'

Meg saw that she wanted to be busy. 'That would be nice, but I haven't got many vegetables in.'

'I'll go.' The girl, plumper than ever since going home and doing little, was eager to be doing something. 'Away you go to the drawing room. Meg. There's sherry and port on the trolley.' And that brought more tears to Meg's eyes, as she saw how Catriona was trying to recreate the atmosphere of Craigie House when its mistress was alive.

Rex sat by her, and they chatted, perfunctorily at first. 'I've been thinking of you a lot, Meg,' he told her.

'I'd rather you didn't, you know.'

He smiled. He had a slow, romantic smile. It had captured Meg last time; she had adored the way it started in his eyes, and lit up his whole face. 'I do know. In fact, Meg, I see completely what a swine I was last time we—were friendly. I just didn't know how well off I was. I want to start again, Meg—but not this minute. Only when you're ready. I swear it will be different this time—I swear.'

She weakened. 'I'm very tired, Rex. How about ringing me next week?'

'Whenever you say, love.'

She stood up to go to the trolley, but Rex was there before her. 'Let me get you something.'

'Dry sherry, please.'

Rex poured two, and they sat again, side by side. Meg had to admit that it was nice having him here. Even though she could never trust him, it was nice of him to be there when she needed someone.

They heard Catriona coming back, then the familiar and nostalgic smell of frying onions. And then suddenly the door opened and a man's voice, taut and angry, said,

'I can't think what you're doing here, Donaldson.' It was Rory Henderson. He still wore his funeral suit, and he stood at the door, his tall frame tense, his blue eyes deep with feeling. 'You're not quite the fellow Meg would want to be hanging around on a day like this.'

Meg said quickly, 'No, Rory, it's all right, really.'

His brows almost met in the middle of his noble forehead. 'I came as soon as I could—I knew you needed me. I finished the calls quickly so that I could get to you. I didn't realise you'd made your own arrangements!'

Meg said weakly, 'It isn't like that. I——'

'I thought the lovesick kid had learned a lesson. You're telling me you haven't?'

Meg turned and ran from the room. She didn't want to have to try and unravel her feelings in front of both men. It wasn't fair, and she wanted now to be left alone. But Rory followed her and took both her shoulders, looking deep into her eyes. The grandfather clock struck one, at her elbow. Rory's eyes were wet, his expression suddenly inexpressibly sad. In the shadowy hall she put up both hands and cupped his face, his warm, familiar face. 'Oh, Rory!' she sighed.

He let go her shoulders, and she moved her hands. They stood facing each other, full of feelings, but unable to express them. She had to try. 'I needed—someone . . .' she began.'

'I came, didn't I?'

Meg took a deep shuddering breath. How did you tell someone that he was a traitor? That you knew he was acting behind your back? That you knew he was waiting to buy your home from around you? How did you say anything to someone you loved so much? She spoke, and her voice seemed to be coming from somewhere else. 'I needed someone I could trust.'

Rory's reply was distant too. 'And you trust—that?'

Meg said sharply, 'That isn't fair! He——' but there was no time for more, as Rory caught her in a powerful embrace, and before she could gather her thoughts he had pressed his lips upon hers in a passionate and breathtaking way. From the depths of misery, Meg felt herself surfacing in the grip of Rory's unexpected assault. And even as she fought him, she knew that this man's love was all she wanted in life. She caught him against her, forgetting her hurt at his deceit. As his lips left hers she moaned his name, and he repossessed her with a force she could never have imagined possible.

Still holding her against him, Rory whispered, 'Get him out of here. Get rid of him, Meg. We don't want any outsiders here.'

Catching her breath, she said, 'I'll speak to him.'

'Hurry up, then. Do it now.' He released his hold on her, and she backed away, still looking at Rory, unsure of her own feelings. He saw her expression. 'What is it? Don't you trust me, Meg—letting him in here on this day of all days?'

She hesitated. 'He was kind, Rory. Very kind.'

Rory's blue eyes burned under black brows. 'He'll say anything for his own gain.'

Meg rallied to Rex's defence. 'Anyone would. You would. What about your clever ploy of sending Caroline here to offer to buy Craigie House? You knew she wanted it, didn't you? But you allowed her to come and upset me, for your own future again. So don't be so quick to blame Rex.'

Rory said at once, 'That was unfair, I know, but right in the long run. We didn't want speculators from outside taking advantage of you.'

'You can't think much of my common sense if you think for a minute I'd discuss business on the day Auntie died!' Then the grief of the day overcame her again. She sobbed openly, and turned away. 'Go home, Rory,' she begged. 'Please go home!'

'It's Donaldson who's going home, remember? You're going to tell him to get out.'

'I don't think so. He's hurt me less than you have,

Rory. You didn't even tell me that the house was part mine.'

Exasperated, Rory said, 'You would have been more upset.'

'There's no need to raise your voice to me!'

'Meg, you're not turning against me, are you?' His voice was gentle, deep and loving.

Meg's emotions were sadly out of control. She said, trying to restrain her sobs, 'You don't deny that you and Caroline Forbes are doing business together?'

Rory shook his head, taking a step nearer to her. 'I don't deny it, Meg. It's not criminal to do business —especially when I believe you'll come out the winner in the end, lass.'

She shook her head, her hair falling about her face in the vehemence of her gesture. 'No, Rory, I don't think you've been fair with me. I want you to leave—I want you both to leave. I can't think any more today. It's all so sad, Rory, so terribly sad . . .' But as he came towards her, she turned and ran back into the drawing room. She heard the front door slam.

Rex stood up. 'Let me——' he began.

'Go home, please! Go now. Ring me—at the end of the week, maybe?' Meg was pleading with him, unable to see the expression on his face because of the tears blurring her eyes, and the strands of hair she had not bothered to put back. Rex came up to her and gently smoothed the hair back behind her ears. Then he turned, and left the house. She heard the expensive purr of the engine as he switched on the ignition, and she sank back on the sofa, emotionally drained, and with no feelings but blankness. She felt very alone. She had trusted Rory until that point—when he had admitted openly that he and Caroline were working together. Even to say that Meg would be the winner! That was too much. How could the victim become a winner? She leaned back, her head against the soft velvet, and closed her eyes. The kitten jumped lightly up and nestled in her lap. In the midst of her misery Meg stroked him, and relaxed a little. 'Not quite alone, eh, Alexander?'

Next morning she woke feeling calm and more in control of herself. She got up, bracing herself to go down and light the kitchen fire, and to cook herself a proper breakfast, even though she didn't feel hungry.

Then she smelt something familiar and delicious. Porridge simmering, and bacon grilling . . . Catriona. Caddy had come back. Meg ran downstairs, her heart suddenly lighter. 'Caddy, my dear, how kind you are!' she exclaimed.

'Morning, Meg.' The girl was sitting on the rocking chair, plumper than ever, but her face had lost the unhealthy pallor it used to have, and she looked glowing and happy. 'I'm not kind at all—I just hoped you wouldn't mind me coming back for a wee while. I miss her so much. I'd like to be—just in the house until you—decide what to do.'

'I'd be so very glad if you would, dear. Your parents didn't throw you out, then?'

Catriona shook her head, smiling. 'Nay, it isna that. The house was ower wee for the family, but—well, this has been home for a long time, and—well, I thought you might need a hand in looking after it.'

Meg sat down and ladled porridge, regaining an appetite at the perfect smell, warm and comforting on a bleak winter morning. 'So you noticed the dust on the grand piano?'

'Aye, I must say I'd like to get started with a duster —when it suits you, Meg.'

Meg smiled again. 'As you know, Jessie is back at the surgery, so I'm going to look for work. In a way, it will be good to get back to real nursing.'

'Have you no found a job, then?'

'I've heard of one—at Dundee,' Meg told Catriona.

'Och, that's a fair way. You couldna get home each night.'

'I'd live in, Caddy. But don't worry, we'll decide

together when I'm away. And I'll not go until you're settled somewhere where you'll be happy.'

'I'm all right, Meg.' Catriona grimaced suddenly and clutched at her stomach. 'I've been troubled with wind a lot. Putting on too much weight, I expect.' The spasm seemed to pass, and she sat up to pass the bacon and tomatoes across the scrubbed wood table.

Meg didn't go to Dundee that day. But the day after, she telephoned Lindsay McDonald at Ninewells Hospital and asked her about the prospective job in Intensive Care.

'Come on over,' Lindsay invited. 'It's no advertised yet, but Connie is definitely leaving, and I'm certain you'd be on the short list. Why don't you have a word with Mr Brooking?'

And so Meg found herself driving along the Perth road towards the hospital. For a while the worries over Craigie House faded, as she remembered the good times and the good friends of her early training days. Only the ache in her chest reminded her of Rory Henderson and his treachery. Why had he treated her as though she were special, when all he was after was her inheritance? Perhaps he had thought she was still the simple school-girl he once knew. Yet she had thought that was changing. Meg gritted her teeth. From now on she would trust nobody. And she would earn her own money, and become a devoted nurse and career woman. It was a prospect that pleased her immensely, free as it was of emotional tangles that only ended in disaster.

She met Lindsay for lunch in the nurses' dining room. They chattered a lot, mostly about Meg coming to work but also about the coming pantomime in Brathay, and about Miles Thackeray, who was apparently of special interest to Lindsay . . . 'You will make sure I can help backstage, like we did last year?'

'I've already promised we will,' Meg assured her.

'Och, that's fine.' Lindsay pretended to be offended at

Meg's knowing look. 'I'm into the theatre just now—I want to learn more about production, so that I can do more for the hospital concert group.'

'I see. Well, if I get the job here, don't expect me to join that too.'

'You will get it—don't say "If". I know you'd be just right.'

Then their chat was interrupted by a masculine voice, and Rex Donaldson stopped at their table, leaning down with interest, to the envy of a tableful of adoring nurses further down the room. 'Well, this must be my birthday. Hello, Meg. I do hope you're feeling better. Hello, Lindsay.'

But his eyes were all for Meg. She greeted him politely. It was a good feeling to know that he no longer had the slightest power over her emotions. 'I have an appointment to see the Chief Nursing Officer,' she told him.

'That's great news, Meg.' Lindsay tactfully withdrew, pleading workload. Rex waved to her absently and took her place opposite Meg. 'Look, I've got a list now. But it's only varicose veins, and a couple of lipomas. I'll get the registrar to take over, and see you in the foyer in half an hour.'

'But——' Meg began.

'Please. Let me show you around, see what new equipment we've got, meet some of the new people —have dinner with me tonight——'

'Hey, wait a minute! I didn't come for a social life, Rex. And I've told you—I'm not available in the way you want.' Meg smiled at him, expecting him to withdraw his invitation at her outspoken admission.

'You have no idea what I want, Meg Mackenzie.' His grey eyes were amused and totally unperturbed. 'Have dinner with me, and I swear that's all I want—your company.'

'You've developed some new lines in seduction since I last worked here,' she laughed.

'Oh, Meg, you've changed so much! But it's no line, I promise.'

'Look, let me see Mr Brooking, and then we can decide later what to do.'

'OK by me,' he shrugged. 'Just make sure you meet me in the main foyer—there are some fantastic new machines you really ought to know about if you're to get that job.'

'You've talked me into it!' Meg smiled.

Rex proved yet again how skilful he was at conversation. They took a leisurely stroll around the new installations in the X-ray and diagnostic departments. Meg was introduced to several new Sisters and consultants, amongst them the new chief of the surgical unit where she used to work. They had tea in the doctors' lounge, and Meg had a brief chat to the Chief Nursing Officer, who without making any promises, assured Meg that her application would be received with interest. Before she knew it darkness had fallen, and the idea of a relaxed dinner with Rex began to sound more and more attractive.

In Rex's modern apartment they sat informally on the floor with drinks and records. 'You see how easy it is to slip back into hospital life,' said Rex.

Meg laughed. 'It looks as though I've slipped back into your flat, not hospital life, Rex! And I've no intention of hanging around here—even if I get the job.'

'Brathay is a small town, Meg. Rory Henderson is a small-town GP. I can see that there's been something between you, but believe me, he isn't serious about you—I could tell. I believe he feels he has to look after you. He doesn't see how you've changed—how you don't need anyone to tell you what to do these days.'

'You're either a mind-reader, Rex, or you have the most subtle ability to judge your women, to say exactly what they want to hear,' said Meg wryly.

'What's with this "women"? I haven't got any woman. I just invited you round because I like being with you. I admire you very much. And I also think that it would do you good to get away from that claustrophobic little town for a while.'

'Claustrophobic? Brathay? I can't let you get away with that! I was so very contented there when Grace was alive . . .'

'That's just it,' he pointed out. 'Your aunt Grace was like a family, but everyone grows up and leaves home. This is you—growing up and leaving home. I'm not saying stop loving it—just admit that there's more to life, and that you intend to experience it. Am I right? Rex refilled her glass.

Meg thought for a moment. 'Absolutely right, Rex.' She looked up. The surgeon was sitting on the chair just behind her, and his hand was about to stroke her hair. She said, 'And now I think it's time I went home.'

'Meg.' His voice was no more than a whisper. 'Darling, you're irresistible.'

'Well——' she found herself suddenly hoarse, and cleared her throat, feeling a bit apprehensive. 'So far you are resistible, and I'm going home.'

'Do you think that's wise?'

'Extremely wise, thank you.' She scrambled to her feet. 'Thank you for showing me round the hospital.'

Rex stood up too. 'Do you always drive after two large Martinis?' And he smiled at the look on her face, as she grimaced, then sat down again. 'There, that's better. Now, it will take me five minutes to grill two steaks, and about five seconds to open a tin of asparagus tips, all right?'

Meg shrugged, and smiled. 'Thanks, Rex. An offer I can't refuse!'

They chatted like friends. Meg found herself beginning to like Mr Donaldson. He was a superb conversationalist, once he stopped paying her compliments which made her uncomfortable. By the end of the meal, as they went together into the kitchen to make coffee, Meg was beginning to wonder why she had ever disliked him so much. It was only by an effort of memory that the hurt of his philandering ways back to her, made her strong to resist succumbing totally to his charm and able to refuse to make a definite date to see him again. 'Phone some time, Rex—if you really want to,' she invited.

'I want to.' They sipped their coffee, sitting at his elegant pine table in the kitchen full of gadgets. 'Meg, I'm privileged to meet you on the threshold of your new life,' he told her. 'I want you to be free and unattached, unshackled by anyone—that's as it should be. I want you to be able to lie in bed at night and stare at the ceiling in joyful anticipation of the next day, not knowing what it will bring, knowing that it will be fun—a challenge, and a fulfilment of all you've ever hoped for yourself.'

'That's beautiful—almost poetry,' smiled Meg.

'Ah, well, I know it hasn't been like that, you see. I know you've lain in your little white bed staring at the ceiling and seeing someone's face there. You would listen for his car, dream of his eyes, burn with agony when you see him with a beautiful woman, hope he would come and sit by you in church . . .'

'Don't!' she protested.

Rex smiled into her eyes. 'Does it hurt to say it? Meg, come here.' His voice was throaty and infinitely tender. She went into his arms almost inevitably. He didn't force her; he held her with a gentleness that comforted and understood her. And his kiss was gentle too—almost brotherly.

It was only as she drove home, across the Tay Bridge, exquisitely lovely in the clear frosty night, with the water sparkling in the light of a million stars, that Meg realised that Rex Donaldson had had years of practice. He had a reputation for conquests second to none. And although his words were pure honey, she had to remind herself that they were insincere. He didn't love her; he merely wanted to practise his skill—shape her to his will, until she too was a conquest. She smiled to herself as she switched on the late news. 'Oh well, Rex, I'll not say it wasn't pleasant. But I'm on to you, laddie, and you'll find Meg Mackenzie just a little bit too tough to crack this time!'

As she drove along the lonely coast road, past Fife Ness and the whispering dark forest, she recalled his tender words. Yes, she did stare at the ceiling. She listened for his car. And she felt an electric shock when she met him unexpectedly in the village. Rory Henderson was not going to be easy to get out of her system, and Rex was right about that. But she would try—she had to. Rory had cheated her, and nothing would change that.

CHAPTER NINE

IT WAS the first day of December. Meg and Catriona had cleaned Craigie House from top to bottom, and had decided between themselves that any decision about selling must wait now until the new year. But during the cleaning, Meg had realised that some of the furniture must be worth quite a lot, and the books in the library worth even more. And even more she was determined that Caroline Forbes would not get her hands on any of it. Grace wanted it to be shared between Meg and Rory, and as Rory was under Caroline's control, Meg knew she must undertake the valuation herself.

They were sitting in the kitchen after a good breakfast, discussing the coming events for the festive season. The frost was white on the windowsill, the sky a deep and perfect blue. Alexander was frisking about between the legs of the table and chairs with a small potato he had purloined from the vegetable rack, and Meg laughed at his contortions. 'I think you need an animal psychologist, pussycat! Potatoes aren't toys. Perhaps it's getting to be time for your operation!'

Catriona giggled. Then suddenly she doubled up and let out a cry, clutching at her stomach. But she waved away Meg's concern, slowly straightening up and saying, 'Heartburn—too much fried bread again. You'll need to put me on a diet, Meg.'

'You're certainly a bonny lass,' Meg agreed. 'Are you sure the pain has settled? I'll pop down to the village and get you some antacid, if you like. I promised to call in at the surgery to see how Jessie Peebles is coping.'

The girl put both hands on her podgy stomach. 'Seems to have settled. It—sort of wriggles, if you know what I mean . . .' Suddenly Meg began to suspect what she

131

ought to have guessed weeks ago. The abdomen was swollen in the familiar shape of a seven-month pregnancy! What a fool she had been—seeing Caddy as immune from the usual temptations of a teenage girl. Never questioning her when she went out in the evenings—assuming she was going out with her school friends. Poor child! Innocent as she was, Meg hadn't even thought to ask her if she was familiar with the facts of life.

She said firmly, 'Let's have a look at you, Caddy.' And she put her hand over the swollen stomach. The child kicked, and Meg looked into the simple face. 'Caddy, I never asked you—do you have a boyfriend?'

Innocently, Catriona said, 'Not now. I used to go out with Stevie Logan, but we had a fight. He's going with Mary Airdrie now. I dinna like him anyway, he's ower big-headed.'

Meg shook her head. 'Oh, Caddy, you must have liked him a lot once.'

'Aye, I did—when he was nice to me. But then I went off him.' She stood up and began clearing the table, unaware of the great event that was taking place in her short life. There was no inkling that anything was wrong.

Meg said, 'Look, I think you ought to take it easy today. No more cleaning—you worked like a Trojan yesterday. I shouldn't have—I mean, I let you do far too much.'

'I'm fit and strong—so why not work? My daddy always said I was strong as an ox.' Catriona said it proudly, but Meg went to the sink and gave her a hand with the dishes. She tried to think how to put the fact of her pregnancy to her—but chickened out. She would get Rory to see her.

'Look, Caddy, you know all that silver and copper we collected?'

'Aye.' Caddy gave her a knowing grin. 'You want me to clean it. I've been wanting to get my hands on it. I'll get on with that this morning.'

'Marvellous! I'll just pop down to Harbour Lane. See you soon.' Meg grabbed her sheepskin jacket and ran down the road, wondering just what she was going to say to the unfortunate Catriona. Not to mention her parents . . .

She sat in the waiting room, chatting quietly to Mrs Blyth, and trying to work out quite what was to happen to Catriona. 'Next, please.' Rory was seeing someone out, and he raised his eyebrows as Meg followed him into the consulting room. 'This is a nice surprise. I hope you aren't ill.'

For a moment they stood looking at one another, and a host of memories—the smell of his jacket when he took her in his arms, the anger when he realised Rex Donaldson was around again—prevented Meg from forming a proper sentence to explain why she was here. 'I—well, it's important——' she began.

'Sit down, Meg. Take your time, lass.' He came to the front of the desk, very close to her as she sat. 'Now, I'm listening.'

Meg spoke slowly and clearly. 'Catriona McReady is pregnant. Seven months.'

'Are you sure?'

'I felt it kicking.'

'Who's the father?' he asked.

'Stephen Logan.'

'That yobbo?' exclaimed Rory. 'Unemployed, purple hair, wears an earring——'

'Rides a motorbike and is going out with someone else,' Meg finished.

Rory smiled, and put his hand on her shoulder. It was an innocently meant gesture of support, but Rory didn't know her feelings, and couldn't know how his touch affected her breathing. 'All right, Meg. What can I do?'

'Come and break the news.'

'She doesn't know? Why didn't you tell her, then?'

Meg took a deep breath. 'She'd probably have thought I was joking. We've been making jokes about her weight gain. I've been a fool not to think of it.'

Rory reached out and buzzed for Mrs Blyth. 'Any calls this morning?'

'Only Miss Wylie, and Dr Gregory will be seeing her.'

'Right. Then I'll get along and see Caddy McReady.' He smiled at Meg. 'And tell Jessie to prepare for another ante-natal patient.'

'OK, doctor.' Mrs Blyth didn't connect the name Caddy with ante-natal—and no wonder, if even Meg, who was so close, had no idea.

Rory said to Meg, 'I'll be along within the hour. Will you be going home?'

'Yes. I've just a couple of messages to get.' She returned to Craigie House with her shopping basket, and a slight apprehension. How would Caddy take the news? She was so immature for her age, it was terribly hard to tell. Rory had suggested that Stephen Logan be told the news, but Meg thought it better to ask Catriona first, before involving someone who might be more of a nuisance than a help. She met Rory at the door. He hesitated, as if reminded as she was that the last time they talked at Craigie House, it had been a stormy argument, and she said quickly, 'If Caddy is worried, you must tell her that I'll be here—I'll look after her.'

'You'll be going out to work soon. You want to leave her by herself in Craigie House? A place of this size . . .' But he didn't go on.

Meg said shortly, 'I can always postpone going to work. And I hope I can trust you not to evict us at this time of trouble.' She turned and led the way into the hall. There she paused, and indicated to Rory that he should go through and talk to Catriona himself first. 'That is if Caroline will let you,' she added.

Rory brushed past her, muttering, 'I'll talk to you later.' She looked after him as he went along the shadowy passage into the kitchen. How he annoyed her, yet how much she loved him! How could the two things go together? Meg shook her head and went into the sunny drawing room, to wait until she was called.

She walked to the window and gazed out at the ever-changing pageant of the waves. The sun glittered on the crests of the waves, reminding her that beauty went on eternally, whatever small problems the mortals who lived in Brathay might have. 'Meg—oh, Meg!' She swung round, to be cannoned into by a Catriona whose glowing face was wreathed in smiles. 'A bairn, Meg! I'm to have a bairn! Och, how marvellous! Me a mother! I never even guessed it, but just think—a wee bairn of my ain!'

Meg hugged her, swallowing hard at the sweet and lovely way the girl had taken the news. 'Wonderful, Caddy, wonderful!' she said softly.

'I'm to go away down to the surgery to have my ante-natal card filled up.'

'I'll come with you.'

Rory was standing at the door. 'Just a minute, Meg. You go on, Caddy. Meg will be down in a moment.' Meg already had her coat on, but she paused, as Caddy went off into the cold sunshine, her eyes shining brighter than the sun on the water. Rory came towards her. 'It's an extra burden for you, Meg,' he began.

'What burden is a wee bairn, doctor?' Meg smiled. 'When the mother is as happy as that, what right have I to bring up any objections?'

'But—your job? The hospital job you wanted?'

'We'll cope,' she assured him.

'Who's going to tell Caddy's mother?' Rory asked. 'And young Stephen?'

Meg tossed her head at him. 'We'll manage, I told you. Thanks for all you've done. Now leave the rest to us.'

He nodded. 'Right, Meg Mackenzie. I'll be away, then.' And he strode off to his car, turning once, catching her gazing after him with an admiring look. She went back into the hall, embarrassed at the light in his eyes.

She caught up with Catriona in the surgery, where she had just given her medical details to Mrs Blyth. 'Ante-natal clinic is on Wednesdays, and we'd like you to pop down every week, Caddy. Are you staying at Craigie House?'

'She is for now, Mrs Blyth,' said Meg. 'I'll notify you of any change if it happens.'

Caddy gave a little skip of excitement as she put on her coat after being weighed. 'Meg, you'll have to give me a diet now! I'm to eat the right things for the wee one. Have you any books I ought to be reading? And a pram—we should be seeing about a pram——'

Meg caught her arm, laughing. 'You've a good two months yet, lassie! It doesn't take two months to buy a pram.' They said goodbye to Mrs Blyth, and walked down to the harbour, where the sun shone brightly on the water, though the air was close to freezing.

'It's a braw place to live, Meg.' Caddy sat on a bollard. Meg sat on the next one, and looked out to sea, agreeing with her friend. Caddy giggled again. 'You thought the world of that wee pussycat of yours, Meg. Now someone else will be coming along for you to cuddle!' And she hugged herself, plump arms round plump body, rosy face beaming with joy.

There was a shrill sound of an electric drill behind them, and Meg turned. They were doing up the fisher-men's cottages. Outside was already freshly stone-cast and painted white. The roofs had been repaired, and shone in a blue-grey slate. Meg said to Catriona, 'I suppose it's better to have them repaired than gone to ruin.'

'Better to have the cottages with strangers in them, then to have no cottage at all,' Catriona agreed.

Just then a group of men came out of the Fish public house further down the lane. One of them detached himself and came over to the two girls. 'Meg Mackenzie, I have to thank you again for what you did for us.' It was Murdoch McLeod. He walked over and stood beside her, shaking his head in admiration. 'Who would ever have thought you could be so plucky!'

'Just call it a wee bit of gratitude for when we were kids, and you used to let me come along with the lads, when some of the others didn't want me along.' Meg had known Murdoch since they sat in the same class in school. 'Anyway, I don't want any more thanks, do you hear?'

He grinned, and leaned against the wall, a weather-beaten man with great strong shoulders on him, and a mop of dark curls. 'How do you like the cottages now? They've done a grand job on them. They look just as they used to when Uncle Willie lived in the end one.'

'And Angus Cooper. He's been dead a long time.'

Murdoch sighed. Then he shouted suddenly, through the open window of the nearest cottage, 'Who's to be living here, then, Jock? Have they told you yet?'

The operator of the electric drill stuck his head out. 'Och, 'tis yourself, Murdoch. Why? Do you want to live here? Because I tell you, you'll never be able to afford them. All in one, they are. All three making one house —for someone with the money to buy them from Mrs Forbes. She's got a business head on her shoulders —bought them for almost nothing, she did.'

Murdoch shook his head. 'Och, I dinna want to live so near to the harbour—whoever buys this will be painting twice a year, where the sand has blasted the paint off and ruined the posh brass doorknocker.'

Jock nodded. 'Reckon if they can afford the price to buy, they can afford the upkeep. So it isna yourself, Murdoch?'

'Nay, I'm after one of the new bungalows up Forest Brae. Now there's a bonnie wee house. What do you think, Meg?'

Meg smiled. 'I just wish I could afford the fishermen's cottages. Double glazing, is it, Jock?'

'Triple glazing on the front. I tell you, lassie, this place will be a wee palace when I'm through with it!'

Meg and Catriona walked back, discussing the housing situation, but without any direct reference to the fact that they would soon have to make plans for moving out of Craigie House. Meg wondered if Caddy would qualify for a small council flat, now that she was pregnant. 'I suppose we'll have to go and see your mother, Caddy —she'll want to know about the bairn, so that she can start knitting.'

'Och, must we? She's ower busy, Meg. She'll no want to knit. We'll tell her next week.' The girl obviously had little faith in her own mother's maternal instincts. Ah well, Grace would have looked after her—and Meg was determined to do the same.

After lunch, Meg insisted that the excited Caddy go upstairs for a sleep. She herself took her second cup of coffee into the library, where she had started making a rough catalogue of some of the books she considered the most valuable. The telephone rang, and she answered it quickly, so as not to disturb Caddy. 'Hello?'

'It's Rex, darling. I was missing you, so I thought I'd just say hello.'

'Hello, then.'

'Aren't you pleased to hear me?'

'Don't ask leading questions!' she laughed. 'I'm rather busy, actually . . .'

'I thought you'd want to know that the ICU job is being advertised next week in the *Nursing Times*,' Rex told her.

She breathed out, taken aback. 'Wow! I'd forgotten about that. I suppose I'll apply. Thanks for telling me.'

'Do I sense some reluctance? You must apply, Meg. It's ideal for you.'

'Yes, yes, I know.'

'Are you busy tonight?' he asked.

'Very.'

'Tomorrow?'

'Squash night,' said Meg firmly.

'How about Saturday?'

'I'm helping at the pantomime at the Argyle Hall.'

'Sunday lunch?'

She giggled, as he had intended her to. 'It's my turn to take you out, Rex. So don't leave town, and I'll call you. 'Bye.' She was pleased with the way she had turned the tables so neatly. Rex Donaldson had caused her many bitter tears; she felt no compunction in teasing him a little. He would shed no tears, that was for sure.

Then a tall figure loomed in the hall, and she gave a little cry before realising it was Rory. 'Oh, I forgot you have the key.'

'I should have rung—sorry. You on the phone?'

'No. What is it you want?'

'Just a chat. Is Caddy about?' He followed her into the library, and turned on the gas fire. 'Meg, you'll have to sell up, you know. If Caddy is going to be your responsibility, you'll have to act quickly.'

Meg felt her temper rising. 'If you think I'm going to allow Caroline Forbes to turn Craigie into anonymous holiday flatlets, you can think again! I'd rather take that Dundee job, and pay you rent for your half of the house, and stay here. Is that clear?'

'Meg, are you jealous of Caroline?' demanded Rory.

'What a stupid idea!' she tossed.

'You seem to resent her all the time. She's got a good head on her shoulders, has Caroline. She loves the village, but she isn't old-fashioned about it. She sees the commercial possibilities right enough. But——'

Meg interrupted sharply, 'And she hasn't got a small-town mentality?'

'That's right, Meg, she hasn't.' His voice was rising now too. 'But that doesn't make her a monster, Meg. Brathay is changing, and we have to change with it.'

'You can keep your forward thinking! Go and phone Caird, and get him to draw up an agreement that I'll pay you a fair rent.'

'Meg,' he sighed, 'you're so stubborn, woman.'

'Maybe I'm just learning to make up my own mind, not to be manipulated!'

'I'm seriously trying to help, and you look at me as though I'm trying to ruin you or something. Honestly, Meg, you're so irrational that I wonder if it's you or Caddy that's pregnant! You'll be sending me out for banana and chips next!'

'Take that back, Rory Henderson!' Meg went towards him, her eyes blazing. 'Don't you dare walk into my house and speak to me like that!'

'I've known you since you were about two foot high, Meg Mackenzie, and I'll speak as I think fit,' he retorted.

'To think I hero-worshipped you! What a fool I was. I used to lie in bed at night and think you had the most beautiful eyes in the world. Now all I can see is pound signs, you great Shylock!' Meg turned and flounced away from him. He followed her, laughing, and she turned and suddenly lashed out with her right arm. She didn't mean to hurt him, but she caught him in the chest, and he doubled up with a gasp. Afraid, she knelt by him. 'I didn't mean that!' she exclaimed. And then he caught her suddenly into his arms, and they rolled together on the library carpet. She heard the crash of her coffee cup into the fireplace, but she thought of nothing else then, as Rory's lips found hers and he drew her close in his arms, his breathing irregular, his kisses wild and intense. She had never been kissed like that, and though she resisted at first, it soon became too sweet to end, and she found herself responding with equal if not more fervour. It was so inevitable, as though neither of them had any power to resist the urgent passion that drew them into each other's arms, thrilling to every touch.

Much later, as though in a far-off country, Meg heard a shrill noise. Rory rolled away, his eyes misty, his hair tousled. 'What was that?' His voice was husky. He got to his feet, smoothed back his hair. 'Did you hear something?'

'Was it Caddy?' She sat up. Then they both heard the cry. 'It is! She's in the bathroom, Rory. Let me go and see.' She was up in a flash, pulling down her skirt and sweater, as she ran upstairs two at a time. Rory was there beside her as she opened the bathroom door. Caddy was in a quilted housecoat, and it was splashed with drops of blood. Meg went to her at once. 'It's all right, lass—take it easy, I'm here. Rory's here. Don't cry.' The girl's face became less fraught as she recognised she was in good hands. Meg helped her to lie on the floor, while Rory examined her abdomen carefully.

'Definitely in labour. Get her to bed, Meg. If this goes on, we must get her to hospital. It must have been the shock of learning about the baby. If she has any more contractions when she's settled in bed, let me know. I'll just get on the phone to Phil Nelson at St Andrews.'

Meg got the frightened girl to bed, and cleaned up the blood, washing her hands and face as well, and making her comfortable. The bleeding had stopped when Rory came back, but he saw at a glance that Catriona was still having contractions. 'Seven months, isn't it? Well, the lie is normal, and BP is fine. We must just hope all goes well. I've phoned for the ambulance.'

Meg went round the room collecting nighties, soap and towels and a toothbrush. Rory said, 'I'll go with her, to make sure there's no haemorrhage. Will you——'

'Drive your car behind? Of course I will. Second nature by now.' And they exchanged a look of mutual regard, only now realising their breathing had gone back to normal. Meg went and sat by Caddy, her hand on her tummy as yet another contraction rippled over her uterus. Rory went down to meet the ambulancemen, and they came back with the stretcher.

Later, Meg and Rory sat together in the hospital corridor, while a team of emergency obstetricians and midwives stayed with Catriona. They could hear her cries, but they were more of annoynace at the pain than any real distress. The consultant came to speak to them. 'She's going to deliver normally—just a small epistiotomy. Do you want to wait?'

Rory nodded. 'She only learned that she was pregnant this morning.'

'Yes, you said over the phone. Has she a husband?'

'No. She hasn't told the father, and she hasn't told her own mother. Sister Mackenzie and I are her friends —she's housekeeper to my late aunt. I think we ought to be here in case she needs reassurance.'

'That's good of you, Dr Henderson, Sister Mackenzie. It shouldn't be too long. I'll get Sister to rustle up some tea.' The consultant put his mask back and returned to the delivery room.

It was just before midnight when he came out again. 'A boy. We're getting him straight into an incubator. Do you want to see him?' They went into the room where Catriona was lying back, her hair sweaty and her face pink, but a look of total contentment in her half-closed eyes. The tiny bundle was in her arms, but the Sister was hovering, wanting to take him away.

'He's lovely,' Caddy whispered. 'Isn't he lovely?'

They drove home in the dark, the stars hidden by clouds, along the silent lanes. At the door of Craigie House Rory took out his own key and let them both in. They went to the kitchen, where the lunch dishes had been washed but not dried. Meg filled the kettle, while Rory found a dustpan and brush from under the sink, and went through without saying a word, to brush up the remains of the coffee cup they had broken in their reckless embraces that afternoon. He came through with the broken bits, and Meg caught his eye. He put the dustpan down and took her gently in his arms. They held each other in wordless need.

He smoothed back her hair. 'It's late. I'll make tea, shall I? Or do you think a drop of Grace's malt whisky to celebrate the arrival of Baby McReady?'

Meg allowed a trace of a smile. 'I'm forgetting my manners. Grace would never have allowed you to be in the house this long without offering you your malt!' She poured them both a dram. 'Here's to the wee baby. May he thrive and bring happiness.'

'I'll drink to that.' Rory sipped slowly, his eyes on Meg. 'I say, Meg Mackenzie, is there anything to eat in this rather nice house of *yours*?'

She didn't take offence. 'I'm quite good at scrambling eggs.'

'That sounds good. I'll help.' He went straight to the larder for the eggs—emphasising that he was as much at home here as she was. 'It's a long time since I had a midnight feast,' he confided.

They sat at the kitchen table. Meg waited for another comment about the house, but instead he said conversationally, 'Tell me, Meg, did Rex Donaldson treat you very badly? The first time, I mean.'

'No, not badly at all. It's not a new story. Eminent surgeon, credulous nurse——He's very handsome, of course, and his technique is excellent. He adapts to each woman like a chameleon—never the same. And he's honest too—makes it clear he isn't the marrying kind.'

'Meg, some venom is creeping into your voice!' Rory laughed.

'Not any more, I promise you.' She finished her whisky and turned to the kettle to make tea. 'He was the first man to——'

'To what?'

'To make me cry. And you were the second. But that was with rage.'

'Are we going to fight?' Rory's voice was low and unthreatening. She shook her head. Rory said, 'Do you realise, Meg Mackenzie, that we've been together for twelve hours? It's almost three in the morning.'

She looked at the clock. 'You came at three. The baby was born just before midnight, wasn't he? And we've been sitting here for two hours. Time you went home.'

'Is it? I've never spent so long with a woman before.' He was teasing her, but very gently, very tenderly. 'I have enjoyed it—very much. It could become habit-forming.' He stood up and took his jacket from the hook, wrapping his scarf twice around his neck. 'We never did make that dinner date, Meg. Do you think we could do it one day soon?'

Meg followed him to the door. The night outside was very still and dark, with only the constant whisper of the sea, as it lapped gently now on the beach outside Craigie House. A few stars showed between clouds, but there was no moon. Could it be love's light in his eyes? Oh, if only . . .

CHAPTER TEN

THERE was a robin on the holly tree next morning, the branches and leaves edged with an icing of hoar-frost. A Christmas card scene if ever there was one. But as Meg ate a roll and marmalade, her thoughts were with the new baby in St Andrews, and what was to become of him, his surprised mother, and Meg Mackenzie. She made a cup of instant coffee, then after a perfunctory scrub at her teeth, she picked up the telephone. 'Baby McReady, born at midnight. How is he?'

There was a pause, then the clerk said, 'I'm putting you through to Sister.'

Meg's heart sank. There must be something wrong. Sister Lang wanted to know if Meg were a relative, but when she explained who she was, Sister said, 'The bairn is having breathing difficulties, and he's jaundiced. We'd like you to come to be with the mother. She's immature, and needs someone with her.'

'I'll come as soon as I can. But I must tell Catriona's mother first.'

'She's not very far away, then?'

'Not far in miles, a long way in tenderness. But she must be told.' Meg took her anorak and ran out to her car. It started at the second attempt, and she vowed not to leave it out, now that the severe weather was here. She drove straight to the grey council estate where Catriona's parents lived with three of the other grown-up children.

Mrs McReady was a cleaner at some of the shops in the village, and she was just home, sitting in her plastic mac and carpet slippers over a cup of coffee and a popular newspaper. She had a lighted cigarette in her hand, as she opened the door to Meg. 'Come away in,' she said grudgingly. 'Caddy being a nuisance?'

'Nothing like that, Mrs McReady. But—well——' there was nothing for it but bluntness, 'she had a premature baby yesterday. She's fine, but the baby isn't too well. I'm going into St Andrews now to see her. Will you come with me?'

The woman appeared unmoved—or stunned. Then she took a deep drag of her cigarette and said, 'Suppose so.' She took the remains of a bar of chocolate and ate them, adding, 'Can you wait a minute? I'll need to change.'

'I'll come back in twenty minutes. I've got to discuss the case with Dr Henderson,' said Meg.

'OK.' Mrs McReady was coming back to life, after the news. Meg nodded, and drove back to the surgery. Traces of mist lay on the ground, and scraps of it weaved like spirits among the bare trees and still houses. The sea, ever-present, stretched out like some cold grey beast, innocuous in sleep, but always threatening danger if it awoke.

Meg went into the office, where Mrs Blyth and Jessie Peebles were going over the list of calls. The waiting room was quite full, but Mrs Blyth spoke to Rory, via the intercom, who said he would come out to speak to them. He was out in a couple of minutes. 'How's the baby?' His deep blue eyes were totally businesslike; there was no trace of the intimacy they had shown yesterday.

'Jaundiced, and having trouble with breathing. It doesn't look good, and I'm taking Caddy's mother with me to St Andrews to see her now,' Meg told him.

Rory nodded. 'Thanks for letting us know.' He turned to Jessie. 'That young man Stephen has to be told about this. It isn't ethical for him to be kept in the dark. Can you see him, Jess? No need for his parents to know at this stage. Just explain—and make it clear no one is after his blood? It's just a matter of courtesy.'

Jessie buttoned her coat. 'I'm on my way, doctor.'

Meg went to the door too. 'I'll stay with Caddy if she

wants me to.' The cold nipped at her nose as she left the warmth of the surgery. Mrs McReady was waiting at the gate, dressed in a coat and headscarf. They drove with care along the St Andrews road, beautiful still in its mantle of mist, the sun trying to break through, making the tips of the trees golden, and an unearthly sheen on the water.

After a long silence, Mrs McReady said, 'Ye think I'm no a good mother.'

'I'm not making judgements, Mrs McReady. And I want it to be quite clear that I will give a home to Caddy and the baby, just as Grace Henderson would have done. There's no question of that,' Meg told her.

'I'm no heartless, Miss Mackenzie. I'll see to the bairn, though my man is out of work again, and I've three other mouths to feed, who give me precious little to do it with.'

Meg said quietly, 'That's good of you, Mrs McReady.'

The other woman said, 'Surprise that he is, he's still a part of me.' And there were tears in her eyes. Meg felt a ray of hope; the family were not as uncaring as she had imagined. The woman went on, 'Do you ken who the father is? Our Caddy was never knowing what was going on—I thought that would keep her safe.'

Meg told her. 'Dr Henderson has arranged for him to be told. Caddy doesn't care for him any more, she tells me. We shall have to see.'

Sister Lang was waiting for them, kindness itself, although her manner was strict and efficient. Her tender heart showed through the starch of her uniform. 'Catriona is doing very well. She's a fit lassie, if rather overweight and a wee bittie young to be a mother. She's resilient, and she'll pull through fine and get her life together, I've no doubt. Baby is stable, but still giving us a little worry. Come away in and see Catriona first, then I'll take you to the nursery. She hasn't decided on a name for him yet.'

Caddy was sitting up, still a little tired looking, but

proud and happy. 'Hello, Mam. Thanks for coming.'

'How are you, hen?' The McReadys were not demonstrative, but the mother sat close to her daughter, and Meg stood back, to let Caddy explain in her own words, each word bringing them closer together.

The nurse came to take them to Intensive Care to see the baby. Caddy said, 'I can no think of a name, but Dr Henderson has been good to me. Rory wouldna suit, but if he has a second name, I'd like to call mine after him.'

Meg said, 'His middle name is James.'

Caddy beamed. 'Not James, but Jamie—aye, that's a grand wee name.'

So the three of them followed the nurse along the corridor, to the glass dome where wee Jamie was lying, a small dot of pink flesh, apparently a mass of tubes and a gigantic nappy. His hair was black and tufty, his eyes tight closed. So tiny and so very helpless. Meg was moved. She stood back to let the grandmother see. Mrs McReady stared down for a long time, her pale blue eyes bright with an awakened affection. 'Wee laddie, you'll do all right, so you will, Jamie.' And as she murmured the words, the child stirred and stretched, and kicked one scrawny leg. She laughed with delight. 'He's getting stronger every day, hen, just you look!' And mother and daughter stared down fondly, captivated by the new addition to their family.

On the way home they were both silent for a while, Mrs McReady apparently deep in thought. They were almost in Brathay when she said, 'No offence to you, Miss Mackenzie, but I'd fair like to have the bairn at hame with me.'

Meg smiled. 'You have enough room, Mrs McReady?'

'Aye, the lads could share. That is, if you wouldna mind?'

'I'd like it—truly. It's the right place to be, if you're sure you can manage.'

'We'll manage.' The proud grandmother was so sure

that Meg ceased to worry. She knew that Rory and Jessie would help, and that the health visitor would always be on hand. That was if the child made it through the next few weeks. 'We'll manage fine. Och, poor Caddy—I never even kent she'd away and do a thing like that . . .' And the two women laughed together, at the way things had turned out.

Meg dropped her off at her own bungalow. But a tall black-leather clad figure was standing at the gate, waiting for her. It was Stephen Logan, his bike parked at the kerb, his pale face nervous but determined. Mrs McReady stepped out of the car and went up to him. 'Now, young Stephen, ye ken what ye've done?'

The boy looked terrified, yet he stood his ground. 'I didna ring the bell, Mrs McReady—I thought your man might belt me. But I never kent—she never telt me. I want to do something, to make up—to help——' Tears started in his eyes in his anxiety to explain. 'I should do something——'

'Caddy doesna want you, Stephen. You've brought trouble on her, and ye kent how innocent she was, wi' nae sense in her head.'

He nodded, blushing now, his head down, staring at the blunt toes of his great black biking boots. He looked about seven years old at that moment. 'Aye, I ken,' he muttered.

The woman looked at him again. Suddenly she said in a sharp voice that belied the softer look in her eyes, 'Och, come away in, lad, and have a cuppie wi' me. Maybe wee Jamie should have a daddy—though for the life of me I canna see you as a daddy . . .' and the two figures, one so small and bony, one so tall and broad yet timid, went down the McReady path together, new allies in the long journey of life.

Meg sat for a while, before she realised that her vision was all blurred, and she had to rifle inside her coat for a hankie . . . At first Stephen and Mrs McReady had reminded her of a pair of fighting cocks, eyeing one another before a bout. But before the door was closed she heard Mrs McReady telling Stephen that the baby was beautiful. Beautiful—that ugly pink creature, beautiful and loved. If he could only hang on to his little life, his arrival could herald a new beginning in the depressed and rather pathetic McReady family. Meg wiped her eyes again, humble at the huge change in a situation one simple act of human dignity and forgiveness could make.

She drove back to Craigie House. She felt very small and insignificant now in its great bulk. Yes, it would have to be sold. She was clinging on to it because she couldn't bear any more changes in Brathay. But they were happening, whether she liked it or not. She just felt sad, that the home that held so many friendly ghosts would pass into flatlets for uncaring tourists and bed-and-breakfasters, who knew nothing of its soul and its gentle history.

She called the surgery; it was only fair to let them know what momentous changes had taken place in Catriona's fortunes. Rory and Dr Gregory were out, but Mrs Blyth took the message, letting out an uncharacteristic whoop of pleasure at the thought of Stephen Logan joining the McReady clan. 'I'll let the doctors know as soon as I can, Meg,' she promised.

She trailed along to the kitchen. Again it was empty, the fire almost out. She put on more fuel, and washed the breakfast dishes before looking around for something easy to get for lunch. She had found a tin of corned beef, but no appetite when the doorbell pealed, and she ran to answer it, relieved of the necessity of choosing lunch. Alistair Reid stood there, tall and kindly and welcome. 'Hello, Alistair—come away in. I'm just deciding whether to have smoked salmon or caviar for my lunch.'

He laughed. 'And I'm just calling in the hope that you'll come along to Jimmy Stewart's for a sandwich.'

'That's a wonderful idea. Just let me get my coat. Oh, Alistair, I've got so much to tell you!' Meg smiled.

'You've no idea what's been going on in the past twenty-four hours. It would make a television series!'

He stopped her, a gentle hand on her shoulder. 'It must be very exciting. Your cheeks are pink, and your hair all over the place, and your eyes are shining.' His voice was quiet, intimate. Meg suddenly felt awkward, knowing his feelings for her were warmer than she wanted them to be.

She had to make it clear that compliments were not welcome. She gave a casual laugh. 'Come off it, Alistair! None of that, now—it makes me selfconscious. When I find my gloves, I'll race you to Jimmy's. It's too cold just to walk, my nose will drop off.'

So they walked briskly along the coast road, and Alistair made valiant attempts to make normal casual conversation. Meg told him the saga of the new baby, which lasted until they were inside the Scarlet Flamingo, brightly lit and warm. There was only one other couple in there. As the weather got colder, the youngsters preferred to stay in during the days, and watch television. Jimmy was pleased to see them, and made them toasted wholemeal sandwiches with mugs of soup which took away what was left of the chill of the day.

Alistair said, 'You'll be at the pantomime on Saturday?'

'Of course. You'll be there?'

'Does anyone miss the pantomime? Miss Wylie's dancing school chorus? I wouldn't dare.'

'There's a change in tradition this year,' Meg told him. 'The leading man is a man.'

'I must say I approve,' he said. 'How does he take to the tights?'

'They've had to make some adjustments to the costumes too. But I shan't give away secrets. You must come and see for yourself.' She put her hand on his arm, and assured him, 'It's all in the best possible taste.'

They were laughing together when a group of bike boys came roaring up, and barged into the café with no regard for good manners. Jimmy said cheerily, 'Well, lads, what can I get you?'

'Coke.'

Meg suddenly felt Alistair's hand over hers. In the ensuing hubbub as the boys took their cans and switched on the loud pop music, he said intensely, 'Meg, let me say it. I do love you, you know. I want to be with you all the time. I——'

'Please don't go on,' she said quietly.

He looked down, and took his hand away. Her heart bled for him. 'Just good friends, is it, Meg?'

She nodded. 'I'm so fond of you, you know. But not enough—it wouldn't be fair to you. I'm sorry, truly I am.'

'There's no chance that your—feelings might—grow a little?' he asked quietly.

She couldn't hurt him any more. She said, her voice almost a whisper, 'I don't know. But right now there's —someone . . .' She bit her lip, and turned her face away, unable to face the hope in his eyes.

Alistair took her hand in both his and gave it a squeeze. 'We won't talk about it again.'

Suddenly, in the depths of the row the lads were making, Jimmy Stewart's voice shrilled out, afraid and truculent. 'Hey, what's all this?' And as Meg turned to look, his voice died in a frightened gurgle as five youths closed in on him.

'Open the till. Now!' Their voices were thick and barbaric.

Alistair stood up and went across, completely unafraid. 'Leave him alone at once, you great cowards!' he ordered.

The lads turned and gave great guffaws, pretending to talk posh. 'Oh, my goodness—help, it's the minister!'

The others took up the chorus. 'Oh, sir I'm so frightened of you!'

'Dinna hit me, Reverend!'

'You're coming to defend Mr Stewart, are you, Superman? Well, hard luck, mate. He willna stock snort, so he's gotta pay for such stupidity.' Meg sat tight in her seat, knowing she could do no good by moving. Jimmy was cowering in the middle of the group, while Alistair stood, noble but ineffectual, on the outside of the circle. He made a lunge for the telephone, but a youth grabbed his arm and twisted it so that Alistair fell to the ground in agony. The boys turned back to Jimmy. 'Now—empty the till, and we willna hit ye too hard!'

Jimmy muttered rebelliously, 'Open it yourself.'

'Verra well, then, Ah will.' The leader shouldered the proprietor out of the way, and banged his fist on the till. 'Here, lads—the bag!' A plastic carrier bag was passed over, and the lads scooped the money out and dumped it in the bag. Leaving the till wide open, they grabbed various sandwiches and cakes that were on show, and the leader gave Jimmy a cruel kick in the groin, snatched a bottle of wine that stood on the counter, and laughed coarsely as they made their way to the door.

Another black-clad figure was standing at the door, looking very much like one of the gang, until to Meg's amazement he quickly bent and bolted the door closed, preventing the escape. He then turned the key in the lock, so that the front door was quite secure, and flung the key out of the window at the top. 'OK, you guys, give it back.'

It was Stephen Logan. He could not hope to stand up against the five lads, but he had made a plucky stand. They shouted at him to get out of the way, but he stood his ground, though it was clear from his face that he was expecting to be beaten up for his bravery. 'Put it back, Nobby. Leave Jimmy alone at least.'

'And who's gonna make me?'

Stephen tried to reason. 'Use some sense, man. You're known here—you'll no get further than St Andrews, I tell you. Chuck it back, and get out.'

'I'll tell you what we will do!' The leader aimed a kick at Stephen's face, but he ducked, and took the force of the kick on his shoulder. He shouted in pain and grabbed at his shoulder, while the other lads began banging at the door and kicking it. Someone picked up a chair and aimed at one of the glass panels. The glass shattered, and the boys tried to force through the small space thus made, while the sound of a police siren whined through the jagged aperture. The broken glass shredded their leathers, their hands, and the plastic bag, which ripped, sending a shower of money rolling all over the floor, amid swearing and shouting from the gang.

Meg ran to the door and gestured to the three police who had shrieked to a halt outside. 'The key—over there, by the bin!' And as they opened the lock, Stephen managed to unbolt it from the ground, and the police were in, and snapping handcuffs on the robbers, aided by Jimmy and Alistair, who each held on to one boy.

They were just bending to grab Stephen's wrists when Jimmy shouted, 'Not him, officer! He's the one who saved us.' He hauled Stephen to his feet and shook him hard by the hand. 'Well done, Steve. Very well done, lad. I'll not forget this.'

The offenders were taken away, while a sergeant from another car stayed behind to take statements. Meg shook her head in amazement. 'Wonderful that Stephen came. But how the police knew . . . ?'

Jimmy Stewart had been crawling round on his hands and knees picking up his money. 'Nae wonder, Meg. The till is wired to an alarm. Anyone who opens it without pressing a hidden button gets the police station. I kent they were on their way as soon as they opened it.'

Meg said, 'But Stephen Logan held them long enough. Without him they might have got away.'

Jimmy had his coins and notes on a table now, and was counting it out in piles. He turned to Stephen. 'Here, lad, here's fifty for you, for what you did.'

Meg grinned at the expression on the boy's face. 'There, Stephen! A hero and a daddy all in one day, eh?'

The boy's face was a picture. 'And there was me,

wishing I had the price of a decent bunch of flowers—I was on my way to the hospital to see the bairn when I saw what was happening.'

'What bairn is this, then?' Jimmy was looking very relieved and pleased as he started putting the money in a strongbox.

Stephen answered, both shy and proud, 'Mine and Catriona's. Born at Craigton yesterday.' He turned to Meg. 'He'll live, will he no, Miss Mackenzie? Mrs McReady said he's ower premature.'

'Wee Jamie—if prayers have anything to do with it, Steve, he'll thrive.'

Jimmy Stewart came round to the front of the counter, with a bunch of notes in his hand. 'Then for wee Jamie, let's make it the round hundred.' He turned to Meg and Alistair. 'Well, how about some strong coffee while we wait for the glazier to come and mend my window?' And as the proud father roared away on his bike, into the murkiness of a December twilight, the three sat over capuccinos, and tried to readjust to normal life after the shock of the afternoon.

The schoolchildren started to come in for their crisps and Coca-Colas. By then the window was mended, and Meg and Alistair were just deciding they'd better get home. They walked back, neither of them referring to the conversation they had been having before the bike boys burst in. But it was in the forefront of both their minds as they said goodbye at the gate of Craigie House.

'Goodbye, Alistair. You were quite a hero yourself.'

He smiled in the darkness. 'Not quite enough, eh, Meg? Never you mind, it can't be helped. I'll see you at the pantomime, then.'

'Yes, see you then.' Meg watched him stride away, and wished with all her heart that he could find a sweet kindly woman who would be good enough for the saintly minister. Then she sighed deeply, and went inside. Why did life make people love people who didn't love them?

She fed Alexander, then went round the house

drawing curtains and putting lights on to make the place more cheerful. The kitten accompanied her, glad of someone to chase. Then they went to the kitchen, and Meg peeled one potato, one carrot and one small turnip, and put them all in the same pan to cook. 'This must be the smallest meal this kitchen has seen in a long time!' She spoke to the cat, because the seemed to expect it, and it made the house a little less lonely.

After her meal of the vegetables mashed up with a slice of corned beef, she made good coffee, and sipped at it while she ironed a pile of washing she had found time to do the day before yesterday, when Caddy was still around. The little kitchen was glowing warm by them, with the flickering firelight, the scent of logs, and the fresh smell of clean ironing mingling with fragrant coffee. Meg sat down and said to Alexander, 'Life isn't too bad, eh, laddie?' and the kitten mewed as though in reply.

The bell rang unexpectedly; her heart raced. Could it be Rory? They had parted last night on a warm and tender note. Or was she hoping too much? She smoothed back her hair as she answered the door. Caroline Forbes stood there in the light from the hall, swathed in sable, looking like a film star. 'Do come in, Caroline,' Meg invited.

'I won't stay a moment,' Caroline told her.

'There's fresh coffee on.'

'Smells wonderful!' She followed Meg to the kitchen —why use the drawing room for a brief visit? 'How cosy you are in here!'

Meg took a deep breath. She had a rough idea why Caroline had come, and after thinking things over very hard, she knew she had to come to a conclusion. 'Do sit down, Caroline. I do know that the house is too big for me. Even if I pay rent for the other half it would be ridiculous.' She handed coffee to the other woman, and passed the brown sugar, which she refused.

Caroline Forbes appeared surprised. She must have

thought she had to battle with Meg—and now Craigie House was almost being offered to her along with the brown sugar. 'So you guessed why I came?'

'I did. But I wanted the chance to explain—I'd like time. I don't want you to rush me. You see—' she couldn't explain properly sitting down, and she stood up and walked up and down the little room, 'I seem to have lost a lot lately.' She paused. It was still hard to imagine this place without the wheelchair and its gentle occupant in the drawing room by the fire. 'And now Catriona is going home to her mother. I need Craigie House, just for a wee while longer—a sort of emotional link, until I get used to the idea that I'm more or less alone in the world.'

'Oh, but that isn't true!' protested Caroline. 'You've got——'

'I know very well it isn't true, Caroline, but that's what it feels like! Oh, please try to understand!' Meg steadied her voice. 'Sorry, I didn't mean to shout. I do intend to sell my half—to you, if that is what you want. I know very well you want it, and I know from Rory that you care about Brathay, which is why I want you to have it and not a stranger. You know I'm not wealthy. I'll need to ask a fair price.'

Caroline was delighted. 'I promise you a fair price, Meg. And the furniture too. Some of these pieces are priceless—did you know that?' Meg shook her head. 'So you see, I can help you with the valuation, and make sure you have what is rightfully and legally yours. Is that agreed?'

Meg managed a smile. 'Agreed. You're a Brathay woman now, and if I can't trust Brathay people, who can I trust?'

The other woman stood up and held out her hand, and they shook hands firmly. 'You won't regret anything, Meg.'

'I'm tied up with the pantomime this week, and after that it will be Christmas and New Year. Shall we say the first week in January?'

'Absolutely wonderful! And I admire the way you've been cautious. I only want to be in charge of the tourist potential of the town because I don't want someone with less taste, and less love of the place, to come in and spoil it.'

'I see that now. I've been very emotional—but that's over. It's common sense from now on,' Meg agreed.

Caroline turned at the door. 'Oh, not completely, I hope, Meg. There's nothing wrong with a little emotion —in the right place.' They both smiled, and Caroline came back a few feet into the hall. 'Talking of emotion, you have seen the fishermen's cottages?'

'Yes. What a beautiful job you've made of them. A perfect little family home for someone with the right money.'

'Oh, I'm not sure that I want to sell,' said Caroline. 'I was thinking—neither Rory or I have a proper base in Brathay. Now that he's decided to stay for good—you did know that, didn't you?'

'No, I wasn't told.' Meg felt her heart sinking like a stone.

Caroline looked coy. 'I have a feeling—you know how women can sense things?—that Rory and I may just end up in Fishermen's Cottages. That's what we've decided together to call the house. What do you think?'

'Engaged? You and Rory?' Meg felt turmoil. Only yesterday he had held her as though he never wanted to let her go. And now . . .

Caroline smiled. She had an aristocratic bone structure, and her teeth were perfect. 'Nothing's official—I just have this feeling. Do you ever have that feeling of being—treasured?'

Meg thought of Alistair, and she felt miserable. 'I'm afraid so.' She didn't tell her that it was the wrong man, though.

Caroline seemed slightly put out at the intensity of Meg's voice. And even in her sadness, Meg sensed that she was jealous. She hid a smile. Let her! Just for a wee while, why not? Caroline said, slightly subdued, 'Well, I must be off. We'll get together early in the new year, then.'

'I promise.' The phone rang suddenly, and Meg said, 'Excuse me,' and picked it up.

'Rex here, darling. How are things with you?'

Meg smiled. 'Quiet, as usual.' No point in telling an outsider about all the excitement of the baby, and of the afternoon's robbery and heroism. 'You know what Brathay is.'

'Then good news. I've got two tickets for the Medical Ball at St Andrews. Please say you'll come, sweet Meg? It's always a splendid occasion, and I shall be devastated if you won't come with me. It won't be the same without you.'

Meg gave a little giggle of excitement. 'When is it, Rex? I'd love to.'

'The twentieth, at the Old Course Hotel. Bless you, darling! Pick you up at eight.'

'Lovely.' She put the phone down, and apologised again. 'Sorry—just arrangements for the Medical Ball at St Andrews.'

Caroline said, 'That's the affair on the twentieth? How nice. Rory and I are going. We could perhaps go together.'

'That would be fun.' But Meg's voice was suddenly glum. It was nice to be invited to an elegant ball. But even though Rex Donaldson was excellent company, the glow was already taken off the evening by the thought that Rory had invited Caroline, not Meg. If anything had put her in doubt of his feelings—especially after Caroline's confidence about Fishermen's Cottages—then this latest blow had destroyed whatever hope she had. Rory had invited her to dinner—but again the invitation was for 'some time'.

Caroline roared away in her smart foreign car. Meg closed the door with an unnecessarily loud bang, which frightened the kitten and made him dash upstairs.

CHAPTER ELEVEN

THE DAY of the pantomime dawned clear and bright. Meg was expecting to have plenty of time to do a little housework before Lindsay MacDonald arrived from Dundee. She had noticed some dust on the Steinway; Grace never liked her beloved piano to be dusty. But she had only just begun when the telephone rang.

'Meg? It's Caddy here.'

'Hello, lass. How are you today?'

'I'm home, Meg, I'm home! The ambulance was taking someone else, and Mr Nelson said I was as fit as a flea and ought to be at home making my mince pies.'

'That's good news,' said Meg. 'How's Jamie?'

'Picking up fine. Steve and I will go and see him tomorrow.'

Meg felt a glow of pleasure to hear her friend in such good spirits. 'You will not be at the pantomime, though?'

'Och, I will that! I came home specially. Meg, come and see us? I've got something for you.'

'Now?'

'Of course now. I ken you'll be off to the Argyle Hall soon—that's why I rang now. Come on your way, will you, Meg?'

'Of course. See you in a few minutes.' Meg stopped on the way to buy a pair of tiny tartan trews for the baby, and was at the McReadys' house, with no more thought of dusting, in twenty minutes. Catriona greeted her with a hug.

'Thanks for all you did for me. Will you—do you mind—I mean—to be Jamie's godmother? He's being christened in the hospital. The doctor says he'll be godfather.' Meg smiled and agreed. At least she would stand at Rory's side for a religious ceremony—even if never for the ceremony she dreamed of. She handed over the gift, and Catriona's brothers shouted with laughter and agreed that having a wee boy about the place would be an excellent thing.

Catriona brought out her present. 'Just made this morning, Meg. I ken that you don't do too much baking —and I've the time, so here you are.' And she gave her two tins, one of hot mince pies just from the oven, and one of home-made shortbread. 'For you—and for Miss Henderson's memory. She always liked the first pies for the party after the pantomime. I ken there'll no be a party—but for auld times' sake.'

Meg swallowed a lump in her throat. 'I'd forgotten. Thanks, Caddy. And don't you be staying up late tonight—doctor's orders.'

'No. I just want to see the pantomime. I feel a bit like Cinderella—what with being in the kitchen, and now planning to be wed, and with my ain wee baby.'

Meg drove away feeling sure that Catriona McReady would mature into a fine woman. It was Grace's influence again. She would never be forgotten while the present generation of children grew up, whom she had taught to play.

There was someone sitting on the wall at Craigie House. Lindsay was early! But no, Meg was late. 'Sorry. Just let me put these mince pies in the larder.' She was soon out again, laughing at Lindsay. 'Your promptness has nothing at all to do with the fact that the producer is handsome, single and definitely dishy?'

'Nothing is further from my mind.' They left the car in the drive, and walked down to the Argyle Hall together. Lindsay was anxious to pass on the news that the job in Intensive Care was being advertised that weekend. 'You will apply, won't you? It's tailor-made for you, and it will be great to have you back.' And she took her hand from the crook of Meg's arm to do a little imitation of Louis

Armstrong—'It's so great to have you back where you belong!'

The usual chaos was going on inside the hall. Chairs were being arranged, and a rehearsal was trying to go on, with the sound of sawing backstage, and wardrobe women taking articles of clothing from the cast, to be restitched or altered. Lindsay threw herself into the wardrobe part, making herself useful with a needle, where she could stay quite close to the producer. Miles himself was blithely ignoring the sawing and hammering, and trying to coax more fire from the principal boy, who happened to be a real boy this year, and who was getting 'nerves'.

Meg went to help with the chairs, but she soon found herself swamped by memories, and she sat down on a chair she had just put into place, and stared up at the boys who were hanging tawdry garlands of tinsel and plastic holly. She hid a sigh. How wonderful it had been to come as a child—to see these shoddy decorations as paradise, and the faded pictures of jolly Santas as genuine portraits.

Someone came and sat by her, and she turned to see Alistair Reid, kitted out in polo-necked sweater and jeans. He looked dashing and young, and she told him so. He blushed, as far as she could tell in the dim light. 'I didn't do it for compliments,' he explained. 'I just thought it would be more sensible for humping chairs and props about.'

'Absolutely right. You make me feel guilty, being caught taking an unofficial rest.'

'No, not guilty, Meg. It must be poignant for you —last year you had Grace. You've probably never been to the pantomime alone.'

'I'm not alone,' said Meg. 'I've got you—and Lindsay . . .'

'Who's Lindsay?' asked Alistair.

'My friend from Ninewells. Here she is! It must be coffee time.' Lindsay came up the aisle, looking untidy.

'Here, Lindsay. Who's making coffee?'

'I thought you'd be doing it. Lazy hound!' And then Lindsay saw Meg was with someone—someone tall and good-looking. 'I say, I didn't mean——' she grinned. 'Yes, I did. You ought to be in there helping, Meg Mackenzie, instead of lurking in the shadows with a real life Prince Charming.'

Meg hid a smile, and introduced Alistair without telling her who he was. 'Since Alistair joined the squash club, he's found that it's more or less obligatory to help with the backstage stuff and the ice-cream. You don't want to sell ice-cream to the kids in the interval, do you, Alistair?'

The young minister said gamely, 'Why not? I've come to help.' He turned to Lindsay. 'Where is the coffee waiting to be made? Lead me there. I'm a mean hand with the Maxwell House.'

Lindsay laughed, and held out her hand, which Alistair took, allowing himself to be dragged up the aisle. Meg watched them, and wondered . . . Lindsay was a pretty girl, her blonde hair tied back with a black ribbon, her blue eyes laughing and lively. She was loyal too, a good friend, and absolutely straight. Meg began to smile secretly to herself. It hadn't been a bad thing, after all, to get Alistair to join the squash club. Lindsay was jolly, too, and always cheerful. Alistair would like that, as he had admired it in Meg . . .

Lindsay shouted from the stage, where the actors were taking a break. 'Meg Mackenzie, I'll report you to Mr Thackeray if you don't get off your backside and come and help. This is going to be the best pantomime ever!' And the others who happened to be onstage cheered.

'Coming!' Meg felt cheered too. Memories were all very well, but the present was fun, and she had her part to play. She ran up the stairs at the side of the stage —and bumped into Morag Campbell, almost unrecognisable in a blue overall. 'Hello, Morag,' she smiled.

'Nice to see you here.'

'I came with Geoff. He's working with Mr Petrie just now—you ken, the joiner from down Harbour Lane?'

Meg smiled. 'So he's the one doing all the sawing and hammering? Great. The more the merrier, Morag. Coming to help with the coffee?'

'Och, aye, anything to be useful.' Morag marched beside Meg, saying a little shyly, 'I'm right glad you dinna mind me being here, Miss Mackenzie.'

Meg turned. The girl was looking up to her. Meg tucked her hand into the crook of Morag's elbow. 'I'm delighted, truly. The minister had faith in you, and he was quite right.' And together they made their way to the room backstage, where the Argyle Hall cups were being filled with coffee, powdered milk and hot water. 'No saucers, Lindsay McDonald?' she joked.

Lindsay turned round with the kettle. 'Och, Miss Mackenzie, we're dead refined here. We drink out of cups!'

Miles Thackeray came over. 'Now, loves, just as soon as you've handed your cups back, I need some strong hands with the props. The throne is ducky, the best we've had for years, but it's a devil to move. I'll need at least two men backstage between acts.'

'Naughty boy!' The laughter and good humour was always the same at rehearsal. Miles ought to have been prepared for that one. But he merely smiled, and gestured for more help. He saw Meg, and came over to chat. 'Darling, you are going to do the make-up for Cinderella?'

'Don't worry, Miles. I've already checked, and put the colours I want in a secret place.'

'That's wonderful, Meg. Only, with so many teenagers here, I had visions of a Cinderella with a green Mohican hairstyle.'

'Guaranteed pure talcum powder, Miles,' she smiled.

'Thanks, Meg. You're a brick.'

After more rehearsal, some of the boys were sent out

for thirty-seven packets of fish and chips. Miles, with the wardrobe mistress and the props girl, harassed and chivvied until they were satisfied—or at least sure that ninety-nine per cent of what they needed was available. Meg took a back seat at this stage. She wouldn't be wanted until make-up time. And though she had been planning to take Lindsay back for a snack before the show, she saw that Lindsay and Alistair were talking like old buddies, and had no idea at all of the time. She smiled, and left quietly, telling no one where she would be.

She went down to the harbour. The air in the hall had been warm, and she was glad of the nip in the night air. The lights were still on in the fishermen's cottages, and she peeped in, to see the carpets being laid. There were curtains at the windows now—beautiful prints, just the sort Meg loved. She stared, unashamed. Nobody could see her, and it was a matter of personal interest to her to see what sort of interior décor Rory and Caroline liked.

Meg's intention was to slip into the Fish for a meat pie, but when she looked at the time, she realised she had to get back. Cinderella, a sweet lady, and chief soprano with the Opera Society, was fussy about her make-up. She chose most herself, but she valued Meg for the eyes and eyelashes, as well as placing on the wig in the ball scene. She went into the hall, where, as always, the atmosphere was slowly transforming from utter chaos to excitement, good humour, nostalgia . . . Somehow the pantomime brought out the eternal child in everyone. Even those who professed to scorn such things agreed that one had to attend for the sake of the children. Meg watched from the side. The old story of virtue being rewarded by a handsome prince—the suckers fell for it, year after year. And so did Meg, as she saw the wonder and excitement in the eyes of the children.

Meg and Cinderella shared a small dressing room with the Ugly Sisters. And as the Ugly Sisters were men, Cinderella had to get ready before they arrived. The men were stalwarts of the Gilbert and Sullivan Society, and adept at making themselves look utterly ridiculous. The making up session was hysterically funny, making Cinderella relax, and Meg come out with tears of laughter in her eyes. In the background they could hear the music swelling. Miles came in, resplendent in a green velvet jacket. 'Ready, starters? Oh, lovely, Cinders dear, really lovely. Where's Buttons? Oh, out front—I forgot. Right, everyone, places!'

Even Meg felt a lump of emotion as the music faded, the lights dimmed, and the children in the audience stared, breathless, as the curtain slowly went up, revealing Cinderella in rags, with downcast head, on a stool by the fireside, a broom by her side. A large bucket full of potatoes was by her side, and a large plastic cat squatted complacently by the embers. There was a ripple of applause from the elders, then the atmosphere was sharply broken by Buttons, who had been wandering around in the audience with a large boot on his hand and a duster, complaining that some people were put upon. The pantomime had begun.

Meg went to stand at the back with the other helpers. It was like a family party. Even the sophisticated Caroline sat with Rory and his mother, with Dr Gregory beside them, and Miss MacFarlane, the old schoolmistress, no doubt missing her friend Grace Henderson, the evening tinged with sadness for her.

Afterwards, the boys began to put the chairs back in order and clear away the ice-cream tubs and lolly sticks, while Miles brought on stage a case of sparkling wine. 'All right, everyone, come and get it! You deserve it, darlings.' Lindsay whispered to Meg. She had told her to stay on, and join in the party for the cast. But Meg decided not. She had done her bit. Feelings were still raw, and the memory of last year, when so many friends came back to Craigie House for mince pies and carols, became too strong. She left, with a little wave to Alistair. He understood, and nodded. He was having a whale of of a time. And Lindsay wasn't far away.

Craigie House was lit up by the stars. Its façade was bright with moonlight. Meg stared up for a while, saddened by so many things, yet pleased with the way the evening had gone, and delighted by the way Alistair and Lindsay got on. She fumbled for her key. Tonight she would have supper with her memories. Catriona's mince pies, and some warm cocoa. What else? The sea was murmuring tonight, almost caressing the shore. A great peace came to Meg's heart as she went into the hall, and heard the grandfather clock strike eleven.

Alexander hurled himself at her, winding himself round her legs. She picked him up after she had taken off her coat and smoothed her hair back. She had enjoyed the evening, but she knew she was wise to leave now. She knew time had to be allowed for a good cry, at the way things were turning out. But then she stiffened, as she heard a bang. Someone was in the house. And after Caroline had told her about the value of Grace's furniture, Meg had slept a little less easy, wondering if she might be troubled by burglars. They perhaps knew she would be out—had planned the raid to coincide with the pantomime? She pressed the purring little body of her kitten to her and whispered, 'Desperadoes, Alexander? What am I to do?' The very fact that the kitten showed no fear began to reassure her. Animals were supposed to sense if something was wrong.

She stood for some minutes, hardly breathing, waiting to see if the bang came again. But all was quiet. Meg began to laugh at herself, and walked along the corridor towards the kitchen. Then she stopped. The kitchen light was on—showing under the door. There must be someone there, because when she had left the house it was daylight, and she had put no lights on. She began to imagine a band of black-leather-clad youths, like the ones who had attacked Jimmy Stewart. Yet they would have no knowledge of furniture. Perhaps they imagined she had jewellery. So she did—a little. And she hadn't got round to insuring it, as her father had told her she must.

She looked at the slit of light for a long time, then she put the cat down and took a broom handle from the hall cupboard. Gripping it like a club, she flung open the kitchen door. A man was there indeed, but it was Rory Henderson, handsome in his Icelandic sweater, busy pouring out two tulip glasses from a bottle suspiciously like best champagne. A plate of Caddy's mince pies was on the table, and also a plate of sandwiches that were almost certainly smoked salmon.

'Rory Henderson, I might have killed you!' she exclaimed.

He looked at the broom handle and shook his head. 'Not with that, love.'

He was so welcome, so sensible—so very nice to see. Meg swallowed hard. 'What's all this?' she asked.

He came over, and put a glass in her hand. The little bubbles jumped out of the glass, hitting her hand. 'I felt a bit sad—thinking about you last year,' he told her. 'I know I wasn't here, but Grace was, and I had a feeling you'd be pretty blue tonight.'

Meg couldn't think of anything to say, so she held out her glass to touch his, then drained it. She felt immediately more conversational. 'That's one of your better diagnoses. Thanks, Rory. I—I suppose I'm lucky, having someone who understands what the place means to me—how I'm going to miss being here . . .'

'I know, Meg, I do know. You were going to come in here, feed your moggie and have a cry, weren't you?'

'Yes.' She didn't mind admitting to Rory. Even though he was planning to marry someone else, he was still special. Why pretend otherwise? She sat down at the table. 'I must look a mess. But I'd just like to say there are times when I quite like you, Rory Henderson.'

He refilled her glass and brought her a plate and a paper napkin from the cupboard. 'What about the other times?' he queried.

'I suppose I hate you—in a funny sort of way.'

'For making you sell Craigie? But that's doing you a favour.'

'Oh, don't be so logical!'

They exchanged a smile of—was it friendship? Understanding? Whatever it was, Meg felt comfortable with it. The evening was a beautiful and perfect surprise, and it was kind and generous of Rory to think of her. He said, in a deceptively gentle voice, 'It's because Caroline and I are doing this together, isn't it?'

She didn't answer. For a moment the only sound in the little room was the stirring of the logs on the fire as they blazed. Then Meg said briskly, 'I think we ought to adjourn to the drawing room. This feast is hardly kitchen fare.' And she led the way, carrying her glass and the champagne, while Rory followed with the food. They put on the small lamps without speaking, and Meg put a match to the fire. An owl hooted in the pine trees in the garden. Meg turned to Rory and tried to sound completely offhand and natural. 'The pantomime was good, wasn't it?'

'Yes.' Rory took another sip of champagne, then set it down to cross the room to the piano. The duster was still there, where Meg had left it, and he grinned to himself as he put it tidily under the piano stool. 'You haven't heard me play for some years, have you, Meg? Not since we had our lessons on the same day?'

'That's true,' she agreed.

Rory played *The Bluebells of Scotland* brightly, without singing the words. Meg heard them in her head, though—'*And it's oh, in my heart, I love that laddie well* . . .' She tried not to think, but Rory went on to play '*Yesterday, love was such an easy game to play* . . .' He stopped playing suddenly, and said, 'Funny how so many songs are about love.' He strummed gently, his foot on the soft pedal, playing the *Love Lilt* Grace had been so fond of. '*When I'm lonely, dear white heart, black the night or wild the sea, by Love's light my foot finds its own pathway to thee.'*

Meg sat, allowing the tears to flow. It was both a grieving for her own love, and a farewell to Grace. She sat listening to the music, and weeping for her lost childhood, the safety and wisdom that Grace always provided for her. She was alone now—with no one to make her decisions for her. And soon she had to leave this house too, and make her way in a new job, fresh surroundings. The new year would bring great changes in her life, maybe even sever her links with Brathay for a while.

She hadn't noticed that Rory had stopped playing. He said gently, 'You had to cry tonight. I knew you would, and I didn't want you to be alone when you did.'

'It's kind of you.' Her voice was a little cutting. 'I do hope you got permission from Caroline to be here.'

'I don't need anyone's permission.' He stood up and took a mince pie, bit into it angrily. 'I hear you're seeing Rex Donaldson on a regular basis now?'

'I've been in touch, yes. He thinks I should take the Ninewells job.'

Rory said over-casually, 'Jessie Peebles is transferring to midwifery. We're going to need a practice nurse next year.'

'I hope you find one. You won't want anyone with a small-town mentality.'

'Meg——' he began.

She stood up. 'Thank you for the supper, Rory. It was a nice idea.'

'Nice? It was bloody brilliant—having to remember to get the smoked salmon before the shop closed, on top of doing my calls and saving lives!' He went to the door. 'Sometimes I feel you don't appreciate me.'

She gave a wan smile. 'It *was* a bloody brilliant idea.'

He nodded. 'That's right. Pity it went wrong.' And he left. Meg listened to his footsteps down the path, out into the darkness.

*   *   *

The day of the Medical Ball was getting nearer. Meg knew she had nothing grand enough to wear. She phoned Lindsay to spend the day in St Andrews finding something ravishing. Lindsay was more than delighted, and Meg had the distinct impression that her friend was developing more than a passing interest in Brathay. She exulted in the knowledge. Alistair would be happy with Lindsay—if she would be contented with a man of large heart and small income. Somehow Meg knew she would.

They tried all the expensive shops, with no success. The clothes were all too matronly—even dowdy. 'Where do the students shop?' asked Lindsay. 'There must be some trendy places. We don't buy clothes often enough, Meg Mackenzie! We aren't well up in the new boutiques.'

They were trudging along Bell Street, more on the lookout for a coffee shop than a dress shop by then. But they both spotted the dress in the window, and exclaimed, 'That's it!' at the same time. Then they looked up, and realised that it was the Oxfam shop. Meg stared at the dress for a long time. 'It's no good—I must have it. It's perfect!'

'And it's for a good cause,' added Lindsay.

And so it transpired that Meg sat waiting for Rex to call for her, wearing a delicious concoction of layers of turquoise silk, with a deep V at the back, and a fitted bodice that flattered her figure. She could tell from the look in Rex's eyes that she had chosen wisely. He handed her an orchid, and kissed her cheek with a murmured endearment. 'Meg, you're stunning! I just can't imagine why you haven't been snapped up years ago.' He kissed her again. 'But I'm awfully glad you haven't.'

'That's an interesting point, Rex. Why haven't you been snapped up either? You're highly eligible.'

He grinned. 'I have more fun that way. Shall we go?'

They drove in his sumptuous limousine, playing soft

music on his quadraphonic system. He was such a cheerful personality that Meg forgot that her heart was broken, and enjoyed his company enormously. She had always found him easy to chat to, and tonight their conversation sparkled. Rex led her proudly into the ballroom, where an eightsome reel was in energetic progress. 'We'll sit this one out. I want to introduce you to some of my colleagues—show you off.'

The room was crowded. The music got louder. Meg enjoyed dancing, and she became more bubbly as the night went on, and the compliments kept on coming. —She realised that she felt just like Cinderella at the ball in the pantomime—transformed into a beauty for one night. She even whispered to Rex, 'I do hope it doesn't all come to an end at midnight.'

'Midnight? We go on all night, darling. There's hot soup at four, and breakfast served from seven.'

'What will you do if my dress turns to rags?'

He laughed. 'The way we're dancing, it probably will!' And he drew her close against him, murmuring, 'I've never been the escort of the best-looking girl in the room before.'

'You aren't tonight. What do you think of the dark lady?' Caroline Forbes had just walked past, gorgeous in slim-fitting white, run through with silver thread. Rex's eyes opened a little wider. Meg smiled, and he hugged her again and said, 'A bit on the bony side, I'd say.' But she noticed that his eyes followed Caroline as she rejoined her partner. Rex said, 'She's with Henderson, isn't she?'

But it was Meg's turn to stare. Rory was in full Highland evening dress, and he was magnificent. He hadn't seen her, being busy chatting with a group of friends. Rex nudged her, 'Earth to Meg?' and she turned away, apologising for letting her attention wander.

But then supper was served in the luxurious dining room. The lighting was better in there, and it was inevitable that the two couples should run into one another. Meg said haltingly, 'You know Rory, don't you, Rex? And this is Caroline Forbes.'

Rex put down his plate of baked salmon and spiced turkey. He held out his hand, and when Caroline gave hers, he bent, raised it to his lips, and murmured, 'Perfect. You will promise to dance with me, Caroline?'

Meg hid a smile. What laid-on charm! Then suddenly she saw that Rory was trying not to laugh too, and they shared the moment, looking into one another's eyes with a sudden uncontrived intimacy. In a second, he had moved round to stand close to her, and while Caroline and Rex exchanged polite remarks, he whispered, 'Well, are you enjoying dancing with the eminent surgeon?'

'Very much.' But Meg couldn't hide her admiration for her old friend. 'Rory, you look smashing—just like young Lochinvar, or someone like that.'

He grinned. 'If I had a white horse, I'd sweep you up into the saddle and back to my castle.'

'What a pity you're only on your legs.' She looked up with a wicked glance. 'But what superb legs!' She was rewarded for her impertinence by a sudden squeeze round her waist, and for a moment the rest of the assembly disappeared, she smelt the warm tweedy smell of the man she adored.

But the moment was soon over, as they were split up by other acquaintances, and forced to chat to total strangers, or even worse, boring old professors. Back in the ballroom, they danced on into the night. But Meg was looking for Rory most of the time, and trying not to be terribly jealous when she spotted him in a very close clinch with his lovely partner.

It was dawn when Rex drove her back to Craigie House. They were quiet on the journey home, exhausted by the unfamiliar activity. At the gate Rex said, 'My little friend, your eyes are closing.'

She opened them. 'Coffee, Rex?'

'I'd love it, but I wouldn't be so cruel. Go on and sleep, love. See you soon.'

Meg looked down at her turquoise dress, crumpled now after the journey. 'It didn't turn to rags after all.'

He laughed. 'You looked lovely, Meg. Your friend Caroline was a teeny bit naughty—she said you'd got it from the Oxfam shop. Bit of a wag, isn't she?'

Meg was suddenly awake. She opened the door. 'Thank you for taking me—I enjoyed it.' Nearly all, she almost added. But Rex was not to know how Caroline had ruined the whole evening.

He drove away, sensing that she had no more to say. Meg watched the car as it disappeared into the morning haze, then she turned and looked out towards the misty horizon. Her beloved breakers were washing in, singing and soothing her thoughts, reminding her that one unkind remark ought not to spoil all the tens of compliments she had received that night.

But somehow, it did.

CHAPTER TWELVE

MEG was feeling restless. Now that she had made up her mind to sell the house, to move out of Brathay and take a nursing job, she wanted to get on with it. She had told Caroline Forbes she would contact her in January. But she was feeling a deep resentment of Caroline, a wish to get away from her altogether. She had seen little of Rory except at the kirk on Sundays. It was the depths of bleak midwinter, and Meg's heart knew it all too well.

The rain was beating down, cold rain that felt like points of ice on her face. She had to go down to Harbour Lane to buy a loaf of bread, still hot from the oven. She didn't take the car—the walk would pass the time. But as she came out from the baker's, the rain and wind gusted and came down harder. And she ran into the shelter of the porch of the fishermen's cottages.

She had been there for five minutes, staring out at the sheets of water, at the wild grey sea, throwing itself in the squalls into huge breakers edged with white, flinging chill spray over the harbour wall, high into the pewter sky. A man, pulling up his anorak collar against the weather, joined her in the doorway, and as she turned she saw with a warm pleasure that it was Alistair. He smiled. 'I see you've bought your loaf. I think I'll postpone buying mine until I can be sure it won't disintegrate in the rain.' And indeed, the paper round Meg's loaf had melted away, the bread getting soggy.

'If the wind dropped, I think we'd have snow,' she said.

'It would be nice to see the snow. Seasonal.' Alistair looked out at the turbulent harbour, then he turned to her, saying softly, 'Why are we talking about the weather, Meg?' He smoothed back his hair, but the wind only whipped it into his face again.'

She looked up at him, her eyes sincere. 'Sorry—I didn't want to embarrass you. You did propose to me once, Alistair. But you'd not got the right girl.'

'I—I did admire you very much. I still do, of course . . .'

'If it's any help, can I just say how delighted I am that you met Lindsay?'

'I think you mean that.' When she nodded, he went on, 'I—haven't said anything to Lindsay yet. But—well, I think we both—feel the same——'

'It couldn't happen to a nicer couple. You've been great to me, Alistair. You've always been there, helping me, advising me, making me confident that I wasn't alone. I can't thank you enough, ever. But I can be truly thrilled that you've found someone worthy of you.'

He nodded, his eyes gentle. 'And you? You told me that there was someone?'

Meg looked down, inspecting her damp bread in detail. 'Not really. Not in that way.'

'I understand. I know.'

She looked up at him. 'Yes, you do. But life is funny. We don't always get all we want. I shall go back to nursing in the new year, and become the most single-minded career woman you'll ever meet. The only thing is, Alistair—will you adopt Alexander? I don't think he'll want to come to the big city with me. He wants to stay in Brathay.'

'We'll be delighted to have Alexander.' He smiled his unworldly smile and pushed back the troublesome hair again. 'Then you'll come and visit very often.'

Just then the door behind them opened, and the foreman, Jock, said cheerfully, 'This isna going to ease off in a hurry. Why not come away inside and sit in comfort? I'm just brewing up.'

The cottage looked very inviting. There was sacking down to protect the carpets, and the furniture was covered with polythene. Alistair said, 'That's kind. The owner won't mind?'

'To be absolutely honest, I dinna have a clue who's the owner', said Jock. 'Mrs Forbes, now, she's been giving orders, right? But that Dr Henderson, he's been choosing all the carpets and curtains and that. So I dinna rightly ken where I am. Bonnie place, though, is it no?'

Meg agreed. 'It's lovely. And so warm, in spite of the wind. You could forget it was winter in here.' Again Caroline and Rory mentioned in the same breath. She hid a sigh.

Jock passed them both mugs of hot tea, which they put on a plank on the ground. 'Aye, this is better than standing out there waiting for the rain to go off. Just think—you two are the first guests for Fishermen's Cottages, Harbour Lane, Brathay, Fife. You ought to sign a visitors' book.'

Meg looked around at the soft green of the walls, the pretty curtains, the solid wood doors and the genuine beams in the ceilings. It was a paradise for some lucky woman. But she vowed she would not visit when Rory and Caroline moved in. Rory was a friend—of sorts. An old friend, a sincere friend. But Caroline was not, and nothing could make things better between them.

'Aye,' Jock was a chatty type, 'there's many a change now in the old village.'

Meg said, 'There'll be more when Craigie House is turned into flats.'

'Craigie House.' Jock was quiet for a moment. 'Aye, now that will be a blow.' He was sympathetic. 'But it's ower muckle for a wee lass to live in.' He drained his mug and went to the window. 'The boats didna go out last night. Pity help any folk that did.'

'Pity indeed.' Alistair stood up too. 'You'll be wanting to get on—the rain has eased a little. I think I can make it to the baker's. How about you, Meg?'

She took a last look around the low elegant little room, a last breath of the smell of new paint and fresh wood. 'Yes, I'll get away back. Thanks for the tea, Jock.'

At that moment they heard a distinct and loud boom. Jock exclaimed at once, 'The lifeboat maroon!' It was a sound all Fife folk knew well. It signalled drama and excitement and the real nearness of life and death. 'It isna our folk, thank the Lord, but I hope their lives will be spared the day, whoever the poor souls are.'

'Amen.' The minister was buttoning his anorak. 'I think I'll get along to the Crail lifeboat station, they might want an extra hand.' And he was gone, out into the teeth of the gale. He was an experienced sailor, often going out with the fishermen just for the excitement of the closeness of the elements. Meg watched him go. Some poor souls might be grateful for his presence.

Then they heard running footsteps, and someone shouting, 'Doctor, doctor!' Jock said, 'They need a medic on board.' Meg froze. Were the doctors in the surgery that morning, or would she have to volunteer, as she had done last time? Last time she only had to cross the harbour. Today, the lifeboat was going out into the open sea, wild and hazardous as it could be. She clenched her hands, knowing that she would have to volunteer—she must. But so totally aware of how terrified she would be.

Then she heard a sound she knew well—the roar of Rory Henderson's red car. It flashed past on the way to the main coast road, Rory at the wheel, and the lifeboat-man beside him. Meg breathed out, a low long breath. She didn't have to go, Rory was the one who was risking his life this time. She ran out, along with Jock, and many others, who were making their way along the road to watch the drama of the launching of the lifeboat. She found Jessie Peebles had come out of the surgery too, and offered her a lift in her new Land Rover. The two nurses went together, saying little, tense and anxious for the safety of their menfolk.

'There she goes, God bless her!'

They could see the dark blob that was the lifeboat,

intermittently though the huge breakers. It looked like a toy, pitifully, so pitifully tiny in the mighty creation all around it—but boldly battling with the wind, because it was something that had to be done. No one questioned. The men went out because men were needed. Every life mattered.

'There's little we can do now.'

'It's going to be a long time.'

Jessie said, 'Mr Moncreiff will be opening the hall. The town's emergency supplies are kept in the Argyle Hall.'

Meg nodded, and they made their way there. It was always like this. The villagers got together in silent support. It was like wartime, only this time the enemy was all-powerful—the ocean itself. Villagers mixed with the cast of the pantomime, who were seeing to the scenery and costumes, ready for the final performances. The kettles were on—they were always on, and there was always tea, and sugar, and powdered milk . . .

There were quiet snippets of conversation around her. 'The minister went.'

'So did the doctor.'

'Which doctor was that?'

'The young one—young Dr Rory.'

'He's a strong fellow—reliable. A bonnie man.'

'He was born here. He kens the sea.'

'Aye, he does that.'

Meg went over to help the women with the teacups. Someone had heated soup, and they drank that in cups, unwilling to go home when there might be work to do. Someone touched Meg's arm. 'Did Rory go with the lifeboat?' She turned. It was Caroline. Somehow she couldn't hate her. Not when she had come, just like all the Brathay women, to the hall, to be on hand if they were needed. She nodded, and Caroline turned away, her face twisted with agony.

Meg said, her voice expressionless, 'He knows the sea.'

Caroline turned away without a word, and Meg went back to the other women. Women she had known for years, their families and their histories. Caroline stood alone, staring out at the storm, her face now white and still. Jessie came up to ask Meg to go through the medical supplies with her, and they opened all the boxes, making sure that all the bandages and antiseptics were there, all the plasters and dressings and first aid equipment.

They stopped working for a moment, as the whirring roar of a helicopter went overhead. It faded, then another went over, out into the North Sea, to help if they could. But the roar of the storm did not fade, the wind whirling round the sturdy stone hall, howling like a banshee through the trees and between the buildings. The women stood silent, their arms folded, their faces pale, waiting to see what the sea would do to them today. The sky was so dark that it was impossible to guess the time.

Meg sat down at one of the small tables and twisted her empty soup cup endlessly between restless fingers. Somehow it was impossible to think. There was nothing but waiting, in a kind of vacuum. A dark, satanic vacuum, that brought men down to size, showed them that for all their fancy ideas they were nothing if the wind chose to blow them away . . .

Then Caroline came and sat opposite to her. Meg would have moved away, but there was no point. She lifted sad eyes to the beautiful woman who had taken away her happiness, along with her lost childhood, and left her with nothing—with a new life that was still waiting to be planned, never mind built. Caroline said in a distant voice, 'He loves you, you know.'

Meg felt angry. 'Are you trying to hurt me more?'

Caroline shook her head. 'No.' She wasn't looking at Meg, as she went on, 'I just think you ought to know the truth.'

'Why?'

Caroline licked her lips nervously. 'In case—he doesn't come back. In case he can't tell you himself. He was going to, and now he may not. That's all.' Her eyelids flickered, but she still did not meet Meg's gaze. 'I suppose I kept on hoping that—that I could get him to like me. I knew he admired me. I had a sophistication he thought suited him. He would wear me—like a fashionable suit—and be proud of being with me. But he never loved me—never.'

There was a pause. Meg stared, surprised by the revelation. She realised Caroline had never before spoken of her own feelings. She said, 'Do you have anything else to tell me?'

Caroline leaned back. She was wearing a ranch mink fur jacket and expensive wool trousers tucked into leather boots. Her slim body was rigid and taut with the effort of confession. 'I'm surprised you didn't suss me out, Meg. I had to make all the running with Rory —make all the invitations, make sure I was always around saying the right things. I even tempted him into the business to show him how talented I was. I didn't really need a partner, I was getting on all right by myself. Famously, in fact.'

'And now?'

'I couldn't even get him to bed, you know. The first man ever to turn me down. That made him special for a start!'

Meg was still looking into Caroline's face, and from what she saw, that admission was a painful one. She said, 'He never said anything to me. Why do you expect me to believe all this garbage? Are you playing for sympathy or something?'

'It isn't garbage. The reason you don't know now —and the reason I'm telling you—is that he was saving it all up as a wonderful surprise. The house, the proposal, the rosy future—poor devil!' Caroline saw Meg's puzzled look. 'Fishermen's Cottages, Meg—he bought them for you. At least, he swapped them for his share of

Craigie House. It was going to be a splendid surprise.'

Meg said slowly, 'Did he know I would accept?'

'Oh, Meg, do me a favour! Is there anyone in Brathay who didn't know?'

'Me,' said Meg flatly.

'Well, you know now.'

Meg hesitated. 'And when he walks into that door, I've to pretend I don't know what you've just told me?'

'Oh, Meg, can we just pray that he does walk through that door?' And suddenly Meg saw the real Caroline under all the sophistication. She cared. It was just that she had a different background, a different upbringing and set of values. But she was as scared as the rest of them that the men might not come back. And her conscience made her confess—the raw emotion of a woman, as caring as the rest of them when a crisis like this came along. Caroline looked into Meg's face then —a straight look for the first time. 'I couldn't stand you sitting there like a beaten kitten, when you're the victor in our own private little war. If I've spoiled the surprise, I'm very sorry. But it was something I felt I ought to do.'

'I don't know what to say,' muttered Meg.

'How about hooray?'

There was a ring—the telephone. Mr Moncreiff grabbed the receiver; it would be news from Crail. He listened, then came into the room again, looking mightily relieved. 'They've found the trawler that's in difficulty. It's from Elie—a long way from home, aren't they?'

'The men? Anyone hurt?' It was Lizzie Grant, in her tiny thin voice. Her man was on board the lifeboat for the first time, and the lass was six months pregnant.

'All safe, Lizzie. It must be only a matter of time now.'

There was a buzz of conversation in the Argyle Hall now, as the women moved around, uplifted by the news, chatting to their friends, gradually feeling that they were emerging from the vacuum. Caroline said, 'Well, Meg, he's on the last lap now. Once they've delivered the men from the trawler, Rory will be in his little red car on the way back to you.'

Lizzie said, 'I think I'll away home and make up the fire, get something warm in the oven.'

'Och, away you go, hen.' The other women were motherly, as delighted as Lizzie by the optimism of the news.

'You think—they'll make it?' The young wifie was still apprehensive. Meg was closest to her, and she patted her shoulder. Brathay was a small town, every soul in it was family to Lizzie Grant at that moment.

Meg looked up, to see that Caroline was standing alone, a tall and somewhat desolate figure. Meg said to her quietly, 'Do you see what it means, belonging to a community, Caroline? This is where I want to be. Father and I have no kinsfolk here—yet these people will be my family, they will be with me if I need them—even though I didn't ask, they would come to me. They are here for me—and I will be here for them too if they need me. There's no need of words in Brathay.'

'I know.' The Englishwoman stood simply, alone and dignified in her loneliness. She had thought herself a step above the Brathay folk, but now she knew she had been wrong.

Meg felt a sudden pull of sympathy. 'We take time to make friends, Caroline. But when we make them, it's for life. You'll see.' Caroline turned, recognising the warmth in Meg's voice. They smiled at each other—the barrier gone for good.

The whirr of the helicopter roared over their heads, making further speech impossible for a moment. The women went to the window. The rain had eased, and the visibility was better, though the sky was darkening now with the advancing dusk. The helicopter was going out to sea. That was a bad sign—a sign that the rescue might not have been straightforward. But the women were silent, dignified in their distress. They prayed silently, waiting for news by telephone of the progress of the lifeboat. Lizzie Grant came back from the door; she would not leave until she knew for certain. 'Take heart, Lizzie—take heart,' they told her.

Someone put on the lights, and Meg looked at the clock. Almost seven. She had gone out to buy her loaf at ten that morning; it must be still in the Fishermen's Cottages. The small palace that Rory Henderson had bought because he knew that Meg was in love with him, and would agree to be his wife. She sighed. If only he had said something! Yet maybe Caroline was right, and she had been naïve not to see the love in his eyes when they were together—not to see how he relaxed with her, felt at home with her, able to talk freely and act naturally.

She was impatient now for news of the men's homecoming. Last time Rory Henderson had come home as a stranger. Now, this time, he would be welcomed as a hero, a Brathay hero, along with the lifeboatmen who had all risked their lives for their fellows. Meg turned to look at the telephone—a black box on the wall, with the power to transmit the news they were all waiting for.

Almost in answer to her look it rang, and Mr Moncreiff was there to take the receiver before it could ring twice. 'Yes?' His face showed nothing. He put it back. 'The boat is home.' There was a cheer, but it died, as they saw from his face there was more news. 'Two are still missing.' The silence was intense. Everyone in the hall knew that to be missing in this icy sea meant that there was no chance at all. Mr Moncreiff's voice was gruff as he gave the news he had been given. 'Dr Henderson stayed on the stricken ship with one of the crew who was ill.' He looked round, and his look included Meg, Mrs Blyth and Jessie Pebbles. 'They say he was seen very near to a life-raft. They say there is hope that the two men were both on the raft.' And even as he spoke, the low roar of a Nimrod surveillance aircraft sounded overhead, then grew fainter as it made for the disaster area.

It would stay out till the light went altogether, they

knew. There was nothing else to do. Meg felt stifled, and
turned and left the hall. No one stopped her; it was
obvious that no words could help. They could only go on
waiting. She walked towards Craigie House. The kitten
must be starving—she had not fed him that morning.
She opened the door automatically, and the small black
creature threw himself at her in an ecstasy of purring and
welcoming rubs of his small damp nose. She filled his
dish with cat food, and a saucer with cream from the top
of the milk.

She went to the drawing room and sat on the window
seat. Already cars and bicycles were making their way
along the coast road, to welcome the sailors home, bring
their menfolk back to the warmth and comfort of their
own hearths. Some of the car horns and cycle bells were
sounding a welcome, unaware of the two lonely men still
lost in that black sea, battling perhaps for their lives—or
possibly already succumbed to the icy waters.

The kitten found Meg in the dark. With the sense
animals have, he knew something was worrying her, and
he curled up close by her, not purring but showing that
empathy that needed no other communication. She
heard the distant hum of the Nimrod going home, and
she tried to weep, but no tears would come.

Then the phone rang. She dashed to the hall and
grabbed it. 'Hello?'

'Brooking here, Meg. It's unofficial, but the Intensive
Care job is yours if you still want it.'

'Oh.' She could find no words, so deep was her
disappointment that the call had not been about Rory.

'Do you want it? Mr Donaldson gave you a terrific
recommendation.'

Meg swallowed, and tried to speak normally. 'Can
I—call you tomorrow?'

'Yes, fine. I suppose you didn't expect to hear so
soon.'

'No.' She put the phone down. Then she sat by it,
waiting for it to ring. Perhaps she ought to try the

lifeboat station again for news. She dialled the number, but it was engaged. She tried twice more, before giving up and going back to sit in the dim light of the drawing room.

The sounds of the sea began to change and make a harsh rushing sound—the turn of the tide, that so often brought stiller, gentler weather. Meg tried to imagine a small square life-raft, waiting, waiting to be spotted by an aircraft—an aircraft that had already gone back to base . . . She strained her eyes to see anything at all in that thick blackness, but the effort made her eyes ache, and she turned back to Alexander and stroked his warm fur in a desolate attempt to stay in touch with reality.

Into her consciousness crept a low gentle roar. She blinked hard and looked out of the window, not expecting to see anything, but there was a car there—Alistair's car parked at the gate, its engine still running. Meg stood up quickly, letting the kitten scramble to the floor. News? Had he come to tell her they had stopped searching? She ran to the door, switching on the hall light, and opened the door with fingers unaccountably shaky. But then she could only gape in surprise and hold out her arms wordlessly to the stooped figure who stood on the top step. 'Father! What are you doing out in this cold? Come away in this minute.' Behind Frank Mackenzie, Alistair switched off his engine, but stayed in the car. This was a private matter, between father and daughter.

She led him by the arm through to the drawing room. 'I would have come to you if you'd phoned. Is everything all right?'

'No, Meg, everything isn't all right. I'm wrong, and I've been wrong for a long time. Don't you see? The entire village is with you, worried about you, talking about what you've been through—what they can do to help—and your own father isn't even with you at a time like this. That's a great wrong, Meg, and I've come to try and put things right.'

He was frail, but no longer looked ill. He had taken a walk each day when weather permitted. He had gained weight, and his face no longer showed the pallor of illness. Meg knew he must have thought long and hard about coming, and she admired his strong sense of duty that made him come the moment he had made up his mind. She led him to a chair and said, 'It doesn't matter now. I'm not a child—I have to fight my own battles now. I can't run to be comforted. And I don't want you to be troubled by my troubles.'

'I know that.' His voice was firm as he stated his case. 'You've been far too soft with me. You should have let fly at me a long time ago—told me what a selfish fellow I was, a tyrant, old and irritable before my time. You should have, you know.'

In spite of her present grief, Meg managed a smile. 'No need—you're doing a find job yourself. Can I get you a glass of malt? A cup of tea?'

'No, Meg. I promised Lily I'd be back within the hour. I came to bring you back with me, if you'll come. Back to your own home, Meg, where you should have been since the hour Grace Henderson died.'

Meg suddenly couldn't control her tears. She bent and put her arms round him, hugged him as she had not done for many years. 'Thank you—thank you with all my heart. I'll come soon—truly. But tonight I want to stay here—I want to be here until I know the truth. You understand, Father?'

'Aye. I've not been there when you needed me, I understand that. Well, I'll be away just now—but just so long as you know that my home is yours, and never let the folk in the village blame me for not taking you in.'

Meg sniffed and wiped her eyes, trying to cheer the old man as much as herself. 'They were wrong to say that—you never refused me a home. We'll spend Christmas together, Father—we'll show them, eh? The Mackenzies will spend Christmas together, like any other good family.'

'Aye—and don't let Lily Scroggie bully you. She's a braw woman, but since I've been ill, she's tended to take over the running of the house. From now on it's the Major and the Major's daughter who make the rules at Laurel Villa. Don't ever forget that, lass.'

'I'll be along tomorrow—promise.' The grey old house at the other end of the village had suddenly lost its coldness; it had turned into a home. 'Good night, Father . . .' They stood for a moment on the steps of Craigie House, feeling the bitter wind in their faces, but strangely warmed by the unexpected reunion. The wild sea had abated, but it still looked cold and unfriendly. Meg waved to the occupants of the car, as Alistair reversed and set off back to Brathay. The tail lights disappeared round the bend, and she turned tragic eyes back towards Crail, the lifeboat station, the lonely road that wound alongside the cruel sea. When the sight became blurred with tears, she went inside, her cheeks chill and her fingers numb as her heart.

Time vanished, and a new dimension took its place, when all that mattered was listening, listening for the distant drone of Rory's scarlet car, speeding as usual along that bleak coast road. But when it came, it was still all part of a dream, and Meg didn't believe her own ears. The drone came closer. She imagined it to be a helicopter, maybe a Nimrod, anything but the stark, miraculous reality of a real scarlet sports car. How could a half-dead survivor drive a sports car? It didn't square with the facts. If Rory were lost at sea, his car couldn't be here. Consequence—she was imagining it. Her deep love was playing tricks with her hearing, her hope triumphing over despair, refusing to accept the truth, as being too cruel. She had eaten nothing all day—her imagination was over-active, she was light-headed.

Then there was a screech of brakes. She stroked the kitten, trying to decipher reality from hope. Footsteps. She could even imagine a shadowy figure walking up the path—unfamiliar, in a seaman's cap and rough donkey jacket. Then the scrape of a key in a lock. The moon came out unexpectedly from a bank of cloud and illumined the bay, the sea, the beach and the black rock.

Rory called, 'Meg, are you there?'

Without the cap and the jacket, thrown aside in the hall, he stood in borrowed sweater and canvas trousers, dimly recognisable in the new moonlight. A ghost, coming back to haunt the scene of his childhood. But the ghost had discerned Meg, outlined against the window, and he ran to her. She stood. 'Are you all right?' she asked faintly.

He stopped, so close to her that she knew from his familiar smell that she had made no mistake. 'I'm fine. We made it to a life-raft, and they spotted us.' His voice broke as he said, 'I've come home, Meg Mackenzie.'

She didn't know quite how they came together, but only that they were holding each other as though they would never part again, never let go, never leave each other. He was right. Rory had come home. Their tears mingled as they clung together, gripped each other with fingers that dared not let go. He whispered in short, disjointed phrases, 'I knew I'd make it. I knew, because I thought of you—I said your name, Meg. Like a prayer, Meg, I said your name. I knew I'd come back. I knew I had to make it.'

She said quietly, 'I love you, Rory.'

'I love you, my dear life. I never told you, and I had to get back to tell you—I wanted you to know. What an idiot I was to wait! What wasted months we've had, Meg, while I waited to give you a surprise! The house doesn't matter, darling. All that matters is us, and like a fool I had to try and please you with a surprise.'

Meg held him close, so close that it was impossible to tell whose heart was beating more wildly. Then she began to remember her responsibilities. 'You came straight here? Did they let you?'

'They had no choice. I didn't wait, I just came.'

'You must be exhausted, and hungry.'

'Possibly. I wouldn't know.'

Reluctantly she took his arms from round her. 'I'd better give you something to eat.' His arm went round her waist as they walked towards the kitchen. It was as though he couldn't bear to be separated from her. Meg put the light on and went over to revive the almost dead fire. She put on another log, and turned to look at her love, the first and only man she had ever loved, miraculously returned from the grave. She said apologetically, 'I've no bread. I bought some this morning, and left it at the fishermen's cottages.'

'We'll collect it tomorrow, then. You know——'

'You bought the cottages for us. Yes.'

'The grand gesture doesn't really suit me, Meg.'

She tried to be flippant. 'That's no reason for not trying again some time.'

For the first time they stood and looked at each other, face to face. Rory said shakily, 'Oh, my darling, how I love you!'

Meg said, 'Rory, you're worn out. Let me get you to bed, and I'll bring you some hot soup. You need to rest.' She smoothed his forehead, where there was encrusted salt on his eyebrows. 'Didn't they give you a bath?'

'They bunged me under a hot shower. But I told them I wanted to get home.' He shrugged. 'They lent me the clothes. As you see, they don't fit very well.'

She shook her head, laughing suddenly at the wonder of it all. 'It really is true! You really are here, and you are all right! Come with me, I'll take you up.'

'No. Soup here, and then we'll both go up.'

She nodded, and put a saucepan on the gas. 'We can catch up on food any time. What you need is sleep.'

'And you.'

'That goes without saying,' she said softly.

'Meg,' he began, 'I just wanted to tell you—it was so dreadful, when I was being tossed about like a cork. I should have told you when I first knew——'

'I know. You love me—almost as much as I love you.'

'More than that. Don't forget, darling, I've lived in Africa for a long time. I've travelled around. And in the middle of it all I knew there was something I was searching for. Never could I have known that it was right here—right in the middle of my home town. I need never have gone searching.'

Meg poured hot soup into two bowls. 'Sorry there's no bread.'

'Are you listening to my profound words?'

'I am, Rory. Listening, and wondering. After all the troubles of this year—I never knew that I was the luckiest woman in the world. Never mind, I know now. I'll always know now.'

They spooned the soup, only now realising how hungry they were. Rory said, 'I never slept with Caroline. You must have thought, the way she clung on to me, that she was special to me. But she never was.'

'She told me,' said Meg.

'Caroline did?'

'Yes.'

'Good for her!' he exclaimed.

'That's what I thought.'

On the way upstairs, they stopped at the landing window to look out at the innocent lapping waves on the beach across the road. The moon bathed the scene in silver, as though she were smiling. Rory murmured, *'Black the night or wild the sea . . .'* and they held each other very close. It would take a little time before the nightmare completely passed away, but this time love's light had triumphed. It had lit the pathway that brought Dr Rory home.

Mills & Boon

YOU'RE INVITED TO ACCEPT
4 DOCTOR NURSE ROMANCES
AND A TOTE BAG
 # FREE!

Doctor Nurse

Acceptance card

| NO STAMP NEEDED | Post to: Reader Service, FREEPOST, P.O. Box 236, Croydon, Surrey. CR9 9EL |

Please note readers in Southern Africa write to:
Independant Book Services P.T.Y., Postbag X3010, Randburg 2125, S. Africa

YES! Please send me 4 free Doctor Nurse Romances and my free tote bag – and reserve a Reader Service Subscription for me. If I decide to subscribe I shall receive 6 new Doctor Nurse Romances every other month as soon as they come off the presses for £7.20 together with a FREE newsletter including information on top authors and special offers, exclusively for Reader Service subscribers. There are no postage and packing charges, and I understand I may cancel or suspend my subscription at any time. If I decide not to subscribe I shall write to you within 10 days. Even if I decide not to subscribe the 4 free novels and the tote bag are mine to keep forever. I am over 18 years of age   EP44D

NAME _____
                                        (CAPITALS PLEASE)

ADDRESS _____

_____

_____ POSTCODE _____

Mills & Boon Ltd. reserve the right to exercise discretion in granting membership. You may be mailed with other offers as a result of this application. Offer expires December 31st 1988 and is limited to one per household.
Offer applies in UK and Eire only. Overseas send for details.